Zombies

eat

flesh

Chapter 1

Yellow bus

The yellow school bus sat in the school play ground outside it was like a scene from a riot. Only the rioters were dead, and the few remaining humans outside were screaming and shouting as the zombies took them down. Dead hands battered the sides of the yellow bus, and the moans and groans from the dead were just awful. The dead had begun to rise up around four weeks ago, at first everyone thought it was a joke a media circus.

But then the zombies were outside your own houses and taking people down on your own streets. They said once it happened it would happen quickly, and it did just that. No one knew if it was a virus, a witch doctor, an evil cult opening the gates of hell, or a virus from a meteor rite from outer space.

Inside the yellow bus two teachers Mr. Robinson a black man who was born and bred in England, and a woman Mrs. Shields. Mr. Robinson was thirty-eight and had short curly hair which was going grey on the sides. He was a tall thin man with a kind face, and a good smile. He had seen his wife killed by the zombies as they had tried to escape with his brother running to a car. Then his brother had been taken down, and Kenny Robinson had been forced to drive off himself. He had come back to the school to pick up a few things, and had run into Ralph the driver, and Wendy Shields.

Mrs. Shields was a thin bird like woman with dyed black hair and glasses she looked a lot older than her forty-six years. She was single, and when the outbreak had happened, she had stayed inside the school building. The two teachers were trying to keep the six school kids calm they were waiting for the bus driver.

Lucy was a pretty little girl with blonde pig tails she was sitting with her best friend Linda who had dark short hair. Lucy lived with her mother and had never met her father; all her mother would say was that he had gone away. Linda came from a loving family and she missed them badly, and hoped that they were safe. Aaron sat on his own as did all the rest of the school kids he had a crew cut and blue eyes. He lived with his father a bully of a man who ruled his son, and taught him all about the bad black people, and Indians, but Mr Robinson was nice so Aaron was a bit confused.

David was called snooty nose because his nose was always running, he had short brown hair in a face filled with terror. He lived with his loving parents who spoilt him rotten anything he wanted they would get for him.

Petra had her pretty little face in her hands she had long ginger hair which the kids used to make fun of. She lived with her aunt since coming over from Poland, her parents had died when she was young in a car accident. Coming over to England was her aunts dream, and she lived well off the benefit system milking it for all it was worth.

Finally, Gavin the cry baby of the group he was taunted by the other kids for being so, but no one was taunting him now as he sat there and cried. Again, Gavin was a spoilt child and always got his way at home, but at school he was afraid, and cried all the time.

"Shit where the hell is he," Mr. Robinson said looking through the double doors of the yellow bus. All he could see was a swarm of zombies banging on the doors, and not much else. One zombie had a nurse uniform on, and half of her jaw was missing he turned away in disgust.

"Don't worry I'm sure he will be here," Mrs Shields replied.

Mr Robinson turned to the frightened kids and said, "Now everyone calm down we will be off soon and Gavin stop crying."

Ralph was stuck in the bloody head master's office and the front door and back door were crammed with zombies. Ralph was sixty and was looking forward to retirement before the outbreak. His wife of thirty years was dead or rather undead he had left her walking about in the street where they had lived.

Damn zombies had gotten to her before he had gotten home that day. Now they had the yellow bus, and he had been a fool to tell the others he would go and get supplies for the trip. He had a rucksack full of bottles of water and tinned soup and that was it, but it was better than nothing, but now he had to get back to the bus.

He rubbed his fat belly a testament to all the nights he spent down the local boozer and the takeaways after. The best way was to go out the back door he looked out of the window there were loads of the things, he could see the yellow bus not too far away zombies banging on its sides.

"Oh well fuck it," he shouted into the empty head master's office, and pushed open the door. The zombies came at him and he swung the rucksack, he hit one zombie wearing a baseball shirt across the face and it went down. Another reached for his arm a woman with a white dress, and he head butted her.

He ran through the zombies all of them trying to grab any part of his body they could. He then let out a gasp and stopped and looked down a small school kid had attached herself to his leg, and had bitten into his ankle! He screamed and kicked the zombie kid in the head its head went back, and she let go of his leg the wound was only small and didn't bleed much through the sock.

He ran for the yellow bus, and saw the black man pushing open the double doors. He hit the zombies with the rucksack and made a clear path for himself, and he ran onto the bus and the doors closed. He sat in the driver's seat his injured ankle away from prying eyes, and slowly got his breath back damn he was out of shape.

"Okay give me a minute and then we roll out of here."

Mr Robinson looked out of the bus windows there seemed to be even more zombies out there, "I don't think I want to wait even a minute."

Ralph saw the ever-increasing horde of zombies, and started the bus engine and called out to the kids, "Okay kids off we go."

Lucy looked at her friend Linda who had been crying, "Don't worry Linda we are getting out now."

Linda nodded her pretty head and said, "Good I'm so scared."

"I want my mummy," Gavin cried out and Mrs Shields went to calm the small boy down. David wiped snoot from his nose with his sleeve, and looked out at the zombies and said, "It's like a horror movie out there."

"Horror movie my arse this is real and we have to be ready," Aaron said clenching his little fists. His father had bought him up to be tough, and he believed he was tough with his crew cut hair. Petra didn't say a word she just looked outside the window at the zombies.

==

The yellow school bus stopped in a field after a day of driving through ruined towns and cities. They had no idea where they were as they entered the English countryside, but soon found a field surrounded by trees to rest for the night. Ralph was in a bad way sweat poured from his skin, and he felt sick and faint as he stopped the bus, and laid his head on the steering wheel.

"You okay buddy," Mr Robinson asked him looking concerned. Ralph looked at the black man and smiled, "I will be fine just need to get off this bus and have a smoke."

Mr Robinson nodded his head, but the man looked ill with his pale face and sweaty skin.

"My dad will come and get us all he is well hard," Aaron said to the group.

"I want my mummy," Cried Gavin as David let a long trail of snoot go over his mouth before he wiped it with his short sleeve.

"I want my mummy and daddy too," Linda sobbed and Lucy put her small arm round her friend's shoulders.

"Don't worry Linda, we will find them all soon."

Mr Robinson looked at Mrs Shields a worried look on his face, "We don't even know where we are," he whispered to her.

She nodded her head, "Yes I know but we have to stay calm for the kids."

Ralph rested against a tree and sighed he was too weak to get a cigarette out his whole body was burning up, and his muscles ached so badly.

"Oh god I feel like death warmed up."

He tried to move his arm, but it hurt so much and he sobbed in pain. He thought of his wife such a kind hearted person, and they had been happy even having no kids of their own. He should have killed her, but he just couldn't do it and he left her walking around as a zombie.

"I can see you my love and I will be joining you soon," he closed his eyes, and his head slumped to one side.

Petra put her hand up and Mrs Shields came over to her the poor kid had hardly said a word since the trip had begun.

"What is it my darling," Mrs Shields said putting a hand through the girls long ginger hair and smiling at her.

"I need to pee Mrs Shields," she whispered to the teacher.

"Okay come with me."

The girl took the teachers hand and walked down the aisle of the bus.

"Mrs Shields, I need to go too," Linda said.

"Okay kids I will take the girls and if the boys want to go to toilet Mr Robinson will take them after."

"Good I could do with a slash," Aaron said smiling.

"Okay Aaron less of that language," Mrs Shields said looking daggers at the boy.

Mrs Shields waited while the two girls went over by a tree to pee the night was chilly, and she hugged her arms round her body.

Petra rounded the tree with Linda and said, "I don't know if a can pee with you looking at me."

"I won't look we turn our backs on each other okay."

"Okay then."

The two young girls began to pee onto the grass as a dark shape came out of the night. Petra screamed as the shape grabbed her and pulled her up onto her feet!

Ralphs dead eyes looked into hers, and she screamed again as he took a bite out of her young slender throat. Linda screamed it all happened so quickly, and she felt blood spray onto her from her friend's body, and screamed even more. Mrs Shields raced over and saw the dead child being eaten by the dark shape Linda was nowhere to be seen. Linda was so scared that she ran head first into a tree trunk and went back dead onto her back.

"Mr Robinson," Mrs Shields screamed as the form of the dead man got to his feet and stumbled over towards her, she backed away and screamed as Mr Robinson grabbed her from behind.

"Go back to the bus and close the door now," he shouted at her she ran away towards the bus. The zombie came into the moon light, and Mr Robinson gasped as he saw that it was Ralph the driver.

"Holy shit," he cried out and looked for a weapon.

He saw a stone a large one and picked it up and held it over his head as the zombie got nearer. He crashed the stone onto the head of Ralph, and then bought it down again and again. Blood covered his white shirt as the fresh zombie finally hit the floor and stopped moving. Mr Robinson went to the body of Petra, but she was dead he looked into the forest of trees and called.

"Linda," but there was no reply.

He walked into the trees and didn't have to go far until he saw her lifeless body.

==

Mr Robinson had to drive the bus, and as they pulled away, he saw the two forms of the little girls they had come back as zombies. He let out a gasp, but no one else on the bus saw the sight and he wasn't going to stop and kill them it was safer to stay inside the bus. He drove until the afternoon passing farm houses with zombies walking around, and then they hit a motorway.

At first the going was good he had to manoeuvre through the parked cars, but then as the neared a bridge the way was blocked by cars. If you had a motor bike it would have been fine even a small car, but not a bus that was not getting through the gap.

"Why have we stopped?" Mrs Shields asked.

He pointed to the road block.

"I guess we turn back," she said.

"We haven't got much fuel," he said looking at the almost empty fuel gage.

"My dad will kick the zombie's arses," Aaron said the kids had been quiet the loss of the two girls hitting them hard.

Lucy who was sad Linda had been her friend looked at Aaron, "Your dad is probably dead like all of our dads and mums."

Aaron looked at Lucy and the hard words hit home, and the boy with the crew cut began to cry. David wiped away snoot from his nose and said, "Why did you say that?"

"Because its true snoot boy," she spat at him.

Gavin began to cry, "Don't say that my mummy is fine."

"No, she isn't you cry baby," she hissed at him.

"Okay enough," Mrs Shields said coming down the aisle.

"She is being mean Mrs Shields," David said.

"Why have we stopped," Aaron said wiping tears away from his face.

==

"There is no point in turning back we won't get far I say we siphon gas out of cars I got a piece of tubing in the back," Mr Robinson said.

"Okay but let's try and be quick," Mrs Shields said looking out at the broken-down cars, they couldn't see any zombies close by.

"Okay kids we are going outside and we won't be long," Mr Robinson said to them his hair looked greyer.

"Why sir," Aaron said looking frightened.

"We need gas son otherwise we are going nowhere."

"Okay sir I will look after them," Lucy said smiling at the teacher.

"Good girl you do that."

The two teachers opened the door and went outside the air was cool on their faces.

"Okay let's go over by the bridge," they walked on he had the rubber tube and she held a couple of empty water bottles. The bridge loomed over them as they went under.

"Okay let's make a start," he said to her and began to unscrew a petrol top.

He put in the rubber tube and put it to his lips he spat onto the road way, "That's got it," he smiled at the other teacher.

"I need to pee Kenny."

"You go ahead Wendy, but be careful."

"I will be don't worry."

They had no weapons and Kenny thought once they are back, the next trip they would look for weapons too. Wendy went behind a car and dropped her panties to her ankles, and let out a long stream of piss, she had been breaking her neck.

The zombie came out of the car window it had been motionless for so long, and now it was awake as the sound outside brought it round. The zombie slid out of the open car window it was a slight old man with no hair, and a jagged hole in his stomach. The zombie fell on top of Wendy, and she screamed as she went down with the dead body on top of her.

She hit the zombie in the face and its nose collapsed inwards the smell was over powering, and she struggled to catch her breath. The zombie bit down and chopped off two of her fingers she screamed again as blood erupted out of the stumps. She saw Kenny racing over, but all of the noise had woken the slumbering zombies, and he was surrounded.

The old zombie took a chunk out of her arm and she screamed again and hit him blood spraying over his lifeless face from her finger stumps, and the zombies head went back but she saw Kenny being taken down by a group of zombies, and then blood spurted up into the air she cried out, "Kenny no."

Then she closed her eyes as the horde of zombies turned their attention on her.

==

"Shit I see zombies coming this way," Aaron said looking out of the bus window.

"Right, everyone duck down if they don't see us, they will walk past," Lucy said taking control.

David ducks his head down, and wiped snoot from his nose.

"Where are the teachers," he said he was scared as hell.

"I don't like this they should have been back by now," Gavin sobbed.

"Look I'm in charge now," Lucy said, "Be quiet and the zombies will go away," she hissed at them all.

Not one of the kids questioned her, and they all ducked down and remained quiet. Gavin went to the front of the bus all seemed quiet now.

"Gavin, you look out the front Aaron the back," Lucy ordered them as she looked out the side windows.

"They are back," Gavin sobbed in delight and opened the double bus doors. Then he screamed as the thing that used to be Mr Robinson grabbed his shirt, and pulled the boy into a deadly embrace!

Blood ran down the small boy's body as the zombie chomped on the boy's throat and shoulders. Gavin slumped dead in the zombie's arms and Lucy screamed as Mrs Shields came down the aisle towards her. Aaron hid under the back seat sobbing and holding his legs in a fertile position.

Lucy cried as Mrs Shields took her in her arms, and bit off her right ear blood ran down the child's neck. David got up, but Mr Robinson blocked his way, and the boy cried as the zombie picked him up and began to eat into the flesh of his cheek. Aaron moaned as the two zombies shuffled to the back of the bus he could smell pee, and looked down at the puddle beneath his body.

His dad would have hit him badly if he had seen him peeing himself like a girl.

The two zombies fell to their knees, and looked at him he screamed as they pulled him out from under the seat.

Chapter 2

Avenging angels

The avenging angels were two people who called themselves just that and both were proud of the name too. Since the outbreak the young couple had taken it into their heads that they were god's tool against the evil zombies. They had both been strong church goers, and hardly ever missed a Sunday mass. Dustin was a tall slim man with dark hair and a dark beard to go with it he had evil looking dark eyes and a sneer on his face most of the time. He was twenty-eight and had been engaged to Martha for two years, and loved her dearly the only thing he did love.

He had hated his parents, and hated the fact that he had to live with them he was jobless, and had no choice. He was glad when the zombies had taken them both, and he had sat down and watched through the kitchen window as the zombies tore them apart in the garden. He had laughed when the blood from his mother had splattered all over her prize daffodils.

Martha was a short girl with long dark hair and a pretty face she had green eyes and was twenty-four. She had lived with her drunken mother, and she too was pleased when her mother was taken down by a group of zombies. She loved Dustin badly, and loved the fact that they were the avenging angles god's tools.

Dustin rode the motorbike through the cars and Martha held onto him as they went round car after car. Dustin stopped the bike and took off his helmet he liked to wear a dark shielded helmet, so no one could see his face when he rode even now. Martha didn't wear a helmet she disliked them, and now the law was gone she didn't have too.

"Look at that," he said pointing to the yellow school bus.

"Oh, my that is so sad what do we do."

Dustin got off the bike and Martha followed they both drew their swords. They had found them in the local gun shop, well not guns as such only air guns and cross bows. They were wickedly sharp, and did their job well.

Two small kids ambled by the bus one with blonde pig tails and the other a boy with a crew cut. Martha went up to the small girl, and put the sword through its chest, and then kicked it over then cut off its head. Dustin put his sword through the small boy's head cutting it into two the two sides flapping over as the boy hit the ground dead.

"You got to destroy the brain darling how many times have I got to tell you," he said and went over to the little girl's head which was still trying to bite, and put his sword in its brain.

"Sorry love but I hate it when the zombies are kids."

"I know but the virus takes them all no discrimination."

She smiled at him and said, "But that makes it twenty-three."

"Yes," he said punching the air.

They kept score on how many zombies they killed, and wanted to reach a hundred soon their first land mark.

==

Dustin tried to start up the motor bike, but the damned thing was having none of it.

"Oh well it's done its job," he said and sighed.

"We walk for a while darling."

Martha looked at the bike and kicked it over, "Piece of shit," she cursed at the machine. They walked under the bridge hand in hand and heard zombies inside some of the cars, but they walked quickly onwards.

"So, tell me again why does god want us to do this," she asked him.

He smiled at her and squeezed her small hand in his, "We are gods tools darling the avenging angels, and it's our job to kill the evil that is the zombies. We keep going until we receive a sigh from god himself."

"How we know when god has given us a sign."

"We will know don't worry."

"I like being an angel," Martha was a simple girl, and that's what Dustin loved so much about her.

"We are the avenging angels."

"Why do we keep count of our dead?"

"We must it's important not to lose sight of what our mission is, all about killing the dead once more."

"I think I am getting it all now."

"You're a good girl Martha and we will do well together."

"Will this ever end Dustin," she said sadly.

"It ends when god says it ends that's all I can tell you."

"Yes, I believe in you and I believe in god our saviour."

They walked and as evening turned into night, they found an old farmer shed in the hills, and after making love twice both fell into fitful sleeps.

Dustin was alone and a horde of zombies were closing in on him he gripped his sword, and got ready. Where was Martha, he couldn't see her at all as he got ready to face the horde?

The zombies came at him, and he saw that they had once been angels their wings now grey and torn behind their backs. He stopped he couldn't kill zombie angels they closed in on him, and then a giant hand came down and picked him up. He floated in the sky for what seemed an age, and then he was put down on a road and he saw Martha coming up to him. Then he saw her sword and she said, "Sorry my love," and cut off his head.

He saw her feet as he said to her, "How many times have I got to tell you, you need to destroy the brain."

He woke up in a sweat and breathed a sigh of relief, "What a fucking dream," he whispered and then hugged Martha close to him.

==

The next day they hit upon a city, and they looked at it from a distance the hills and wooded area behind them.

"What do you think Dustin?" Martha didn't like cities the zombies seemed to own them.

"Well, we need supplies I say we go in and out quickly."

"Okay but if we see too many, we run okay no hero stuff not in cities."

He smiled at her, "In and out that's it," he said and kissed her on the lips.

They entered the city with swords at the ready the shops seemed deserted they walked past a news agent with a broken window. Most of the shops had been robbed by looters, and the smell in the city was bad.

"Okay let's try the supermarket," he said spying the long building over to their left.

"No, it's too big we could get trapped in their."

"Trust me, Martha."

The avenging angels were not scared of large spaces, and certainly not scared of zombies. They worked for God and

Dustin truly believed this, and that no harm would come to them.

"Come my love," he said and took her hand.

Inside it was cool and smelt bad Dustin found some tins of fruit, and put them into a rucksack. Martha went up ahead and turned into another aisle. She screamed and Dustin left the rucksack, and ran round the aisle and stopped. Martha lay in a pool of blood, and two zombies with store clothes on were eating her! He saw a burst bottle of olive oil on the floor she must have slipped on this, she would have killed the zombies otherwise.

He stood there and could hear as they munched on her flesh he turned round, and was sick on the ground. He stumbled out of the supermarket, a group of zombies following him.

==

He started to cry and could hear the moans coming from behind him as he staggered on. His Martha was dead, and he couldn't believe it, not like this we work for God after all.

He saw what looked like an office block in front of him, and made his way towards it. The large window doors were chained up and locked, but he stumbled onwards.

"Hey mister," he looked up at the building someone had called to him. He stopped he felt totally drained and sank to his knees the moaning louder as the zombies caught up with him.

He felt their hands on his throat, and cried out as two bit into him at the same time a deep wound on his shoulder and neck. Blood poured out of his wounds and he felt his life slipping away, and he was glad.

"I love you Martha and I will now be with you always," he said and then slipped into unconsciousness as the zombies surrounded his body.

Chapter 3
Office

Johnson sat at the window in the office and looked out over the city. He was forty-nine and a bull of a coloured man. Before the outbreak he had spent almost every day down the local gym building up his muscles. He was even ready to go into shows, and was training for his first bodybuilding contest when the shit hit the fan.

He was tall and wide with short dark hair and his features were like the former heavyweight champion of the world Sonny Liston. He looked mean and brooding and ready to fight anyone, but the truth under the hard features was that he was a kind good man. He saw the man staggering down the street coming towards the office block, and Johnson opened the window and called down, "Hey mister."

But then he saw the man fall to his knees and then the zombies took him, Johnson turned away and closed the window. He looked at his two companions, and shrugged his huge shoulders, "Man didn't make it."

Sarah was a young girl of twenty-five she was slim with long blonde hair and a pretty face. She had been with her boyfriend when a group of zombies had hit the house, and she managed to run for it while her boyfriend stayed to fight them. She never saw him again and guessed that zombies had eaten him, and came back to where she had worked.

David was fifty-four with grey short hair and a wrinkled face he was slim and of medium height. He had stayed in the office when things got really bad, at first there had been a large group but slowly people left, and now only three of them remained.

They were holed up in a long office with desks going along the window side and filing cabinets on the right. There was a canteen and rest room, and one small office down the other end of the office and that was home for them.

Two doors lead to the rest of the office block these were chained up one by the filing cabinets and one by the canteen.

==

They had locked themselves in when the outbreak happened at first there was a large group, but then people had started to worry and panic. Afraid they wouldn't see loved ones and family and soon the group went down to three, Johnson and David had been there, and they had let Sarah in who they knew of course they all worked in the office. The only way to go to toilet was to do it in a bucket, and then tip out of a window. There were no toilets in this part of the office they were by the stairwell outside by the lifts.

"The foods running out Johnson," David didn't really like the black man.

He had never liked him when they worked together so why should he like him now, but he kept it to himself.

"What do you want me to do about it man," Johnson said looking at David the man could be a real prick sometimes.

"I'm just saying."

"And the water is low too," Sarah said looking out of a window.

David looked Sarah over man she had a nice body if he could get rid of Johnson, he would certainly have a play with that.

"Who you looking at David," she said turning from the window.

"No one."

They were on the eighth floor so there was no way of jumping out of the window if the zombies ever got in. Sarah coughed and looked at the big man Johnson, "I think we should get a search party going."

Johnson nodded and she carried on.

"We could go down into the streets and look at the stores."

"No Sarah that's far too dangerous there are too many zombies down there," Johnson said looking at the pretty young girl.

"So, what do we do then," David said spreading out his hands in front of him.

Johnson looked at the two and said, "We search the rest of the office building and get what we can find."

David rubbed his chin and replied, "Wont there still be zombies."

"Yes of course, but not as many as down on the streets."

"Yes, he is right," Sarah said nodding to Johnson.

Johnson looked at David and knew the man wouldn't come he was a coward.

"Okay me and Sarah will search the office building you stay and get ready to let us back in."

David was happy with that he didn't fancy going out of the locked office.

"Fine," David said smiling at them both.

==

David lay down on the floor once he had locked the doors after the two, and closed his eyes. He was so tired of all this and living in the bloody office looking at the same crap day after day it was driving him crazy.

"I love you mother and I miss you," he said out loud.

He had looked after his mother most of his adult years and when she had died two years ago it had affected him badly. Now he sometimes saw her, she was now looking after him he was sure of that.

"I know you are close mother."

Johnson and Sarah made their way up the stairs to the next level all was silent so far. Sarah held a crow bar and pushed open a door leading to a corridor with offices on each side some doors open some closed. Johnson touched Sarah on the shoulder, and she looked at him he held an axe in his hands.

"I will go first you follow behind."

"Okay," she whispered.

He began to walk down the corridor Sarah close behind him he looked in the first office it was empty, and had no furniture. The second one was on the left and the door was closed he tried the handle it was locked. He saw the next door was open and went to that a zombie was sitting at the desk, and it looked up at Johnson as he stepped into the room. The zombie's skin was coming away from its face, and you could see the bone underneath. Before the zombie could get up Johnson put the axe in its head, the thing fell forwards and Johnson took out the axe head.

The smell inside the office was bad, and Johnson gagged a bit.

"Put something over your nose," he said to Sarah and took out a tissue from his pocket.

Sarah found a bottle of whiskey and two packs of biscuits.

"That will do nicely," Johnson said winking at her.

"Yes, I think we could all do with a drink," she replied smiling.

The rest of the floor was empty, and they found more drink but not much else.

David heard his mother speaking to him and smiled he could hear noises coming from the stairwell.

"I can hear you mother," he called out. He got to his feet his mother wanted to come in and greet him she was outside he knew it. He could hear moaning and banging now on the locked door his mother wanted to come in.

"Hang on mother I am coming."

He took the key out of his pocket and unlocked the chain around the drop handle.

He pushed the door open, and screamed as the zombies entered the room!

==

Johnson came out of the corridor and froze the stairwell was full of zombies there was more than he had expected.

"Fuck the noise must have attracted them all."

"Oh my god," Sarah said putting her hand over her mouth.

"Right, we go back down to David come on."

Johnson grabbed her arm and started to go down the stairs he pushed a zombie wearing a suit and tie its eye hanging down on its ruined cheek. The zombie fell into more zombies and they tumbled down the stairs. Sarah felt a hand on her back and turned round and came face to face with a woman zombie wearing a yellow flowery dress!

She screamed as the zombie took a chunk out of her shoulder.

Johnson turned, and saw the blood on Sarah's shoulder.

"Fuck it," he shouted and swung Sarah out of the way and cut off the zombie's head. The head rolled down the stairs still chewing Sarah's flesh in its mouth.

One zombie grabbed Johnson's leg and another held onto his short hair and pulled he cried out in pain. He saw Sarah on the ground a zombie eating her face she was not moving. He cursed as he felt a zombie bite into his wrist, and his blood spurted over the white walls of the stairwell. He started to punch the zombies and kick them he lost the axe, and jumped down the remainder of the stairs. He saw the office floor door was open, and groaned David had let in the zombies!

"Oh no man!" he sighed as he got to his feet surrounded by zombies.

They moaned loudly and the stench was awful. He looked at his wrist blood was pumping out, and then a zombie grabbed him from behind another coming for him from the front its arms out stretched. Johnson pushed back and the zombie which had grabbed him fell against a wall still holding onto Johnson round the waist. Johnson kicked the zombie in front of him and it fell back making a bunch of zombies behind it fall over.

He felt pain in his neck as the zombie holding onto him took a bite out of his neck. He cursed and elbowed the zombie, and head butted it from behind the zombie let go. Johnson staggered passed the fallen zombies and went into the office he saw David in a pool of blood on the carpeted floor. Zombies surrounded David's body and they were taking out his intestines, and shoving them into their hungry mouths.

"I don't want to end up like one of these things," he said in disgust.

He looked at the office windows that ran down one side. He was in pain, but he had enough energy to do this one last thing. He thought of poor Sarah, he had liked her and now she was being eaten by zombies.

David was a prick, but he had still been part of the small group why had they gone out of the safe zone into the hands of the waiting zombies. It had been the only way they needed food and water. He laughed as zombies came at him and searched inside the rucksack, he found what he was looking for.

He held up the bottle of whisky and said, "Good health you zombie bastards."

He took a long swig from the bottle, and then threw it at a zombie close by. The bottle exploded on the zombie's bald head and it staggered backwards. Johnson took a run at the window and then jumped with all his weight and might.

He crashed through the glass and fell to the ground below.

Chapter 4

Red van

The red van stopped in front of the office building the city was overrun with zombies far too dangerous to stop for long. Then as the man behind the wheel looked, he saw a body hit the ground blood splattering all over the ground, and a group of zombies closed in on the body. As the man watched the zombies ripped open the black man's stomach, and began to pull out his intestines. Mitch the man behind the red vans wheel made off quickly so the young girl besides him wouldn't see too much. Mitch was fifty with brown short hair and blue eyes he was a handsome man, and people told him he looked ten years younger.

He had been on his own for a long time through the outbreak it was better that way no one to care about. But then he had picked up Mary the young girl besides him he turned and looked at her pale white face, and her long dark hair she was a pretty girl of fifteen. That night he had stopped for the night when all of a sudden, he heard a scream and went to investigate in the van.

He found a farm house and inside a mother and daughter locked into a bedroom only the zombies had got in. The mother was dead, and the daughter Mary was in the wardrobe he had rescued her, and here they were now a few weeks later. She spoke to him, and they got on well he found out that one of the zombies he had killed while rescuing her had been her father. But she didn't blame him she was very mature for her age, and Mitch found himself liking her.

The red van had wire mess over all the windows and the back had a blow-up bed and blankets plus loads of food and drinks. He had always kept well stored up. Mary slept with him but he would never touch her.

==

He drove out of the city avoiding the cars in the street and the bodies, trying not to run over them. Crows pecked at them and flies swarmed over the dead bodies, and the path ways were filled with the moaning dead. He was pleased when they left the city, and the fresh air of the countryside hit his nostrils.

"That man was a giant," Mary said

"What man love," he was concentrating on the road ahead.

"That big man that hit the ground back in the city."

"Oh, him yes he was a big man probably a body builder."

"Yes, such a waste all that training to make yourself look good and then bang you hit the ground."

Mitch rubbed his chin he needed a shave, "That's one way to look at it love I guess."

"It's late let's pull over," he saw a lay by and pulled into it. It was well hidden by the trees and bushes that surrounded it. They climbed into the back, and had a tin of spam and a tin of sardines each, and a bottle of water. They slept next to each other fully dressed, and Mary hugged the man.

"Thank you for rescuing me, Mitch."

"I'm glad I did love."

"I love you Mitch I know it's wrong, but really do."

She kissed him on the cheek and squeezed his hand.

"I know you do love."

Mitch squeezed her hand back and then said, "Good night my love sweet dreams and sleep well."

"Good night, Mitch."

The next morning, they woke up to snow, and Mary wooed and cheered.

"Oh, Mitch I love snow."

"Yes, and it will slow up the zombies even more."

He was pleased it had snowed it had to be for their advantage. He drove off later that morning after a breakfast of tomato soup and crisps. He drove up the country lane then the road widened and he saw a petrol station.

"Great just what the doctor ordered."

"What Mitch."

"We need gas love."

He parked the van by the petrol pumps, but they were not working.

Mitch sighed, but there were a lot of cars about the forecourt.

"We need gas I guess I siphon."

==

Mitch began to siphon and he found one car almost full the petrol would come in handy. He liked to keep three cans filled in the back for reserves. As he was on his knees and he failed to see the zombie coming across the fore court heading for Mary who was sitting on an old chair by the petrol pumps. Mary heard the dragging feet and turned to see the petrol attendant zombie he was still wearing his baseball cap.

She coolly walked over to Mitch and tapped him on the shoulder, he smiled up at her.

"Yes love."

"We got company," and she nodded towards the zombie.

"Okay love you keep the tube in the can I will deal with the zombie."

"Okay Mitch."

He stood up and walked to the red van and opened the back door. He had a rifle which had been his old man's but that was too noisy. He picked up the pick axe sharpened to a wicked point and smiled. The zombie was close now it was dragging one of its broken feet he saw. It was an old ugly zombie its lips chewed away so that you could see its teeth permanently.

Mitch walked over to the zombie, and calmly raised the pick axe over his head, and bought it down on the top of the zombie's head. It went right through like it was butter right up to the hilt.

Mitch withdrew the pick axe and kicked the dead zombie away. He walked up to the petrol station the inside was a mess he could see through the dirty window and the smell was bad. He could see swarms of flies inside, and shapes moving about.

He closed the door and walked round the back and made sure all the doors were shut it was pure hell inside. The windows were covered in dirt and not much sun light got in, and the shapes moved around like monsters waiting for hells gate to open. Gave him the creeps and he didn't mind admitting that either. He went back to Mary and brushed her hair with his hand she took his hand, and kissed it.

"I love you, Mitch."

"I know love."

As they made to go Mary gasped and pointed!

"I saw a man on the top of that hill!"

Mitch looked but he could see nothing.

"Probably a zombie love."

Mary didn't seem so sure, but she didn't want anyone else in the van that would spoil things she wanted Mitch all to herself.

"Yes, it was nothing let's go Mitch," She squeezed his leg as he drove off and he smiled at her.

"Yes, let's go love."

The red van drove off up the road, and disappeared round a bend in the road.

Chapter 5

Mole man

The mole man Rubin Tate had picked up the nick name many years ago when he had been in a young offenders' prison. He was inside for robbing a news agent, and was a wild boy when he was a youngster, and had even punched a policeman who had arrested him. One day the prison guards and thrown him inside a green house and locked the door laughing at him and saying they would be back the next day.

He had tunnelled his way out and ever since then he had been known as the mole man. The guards couldn't believe it when they saw him running away, a few hours later they caught him, and then they saw the tunnel. It was a victory for the boys in the prison, and he was soon a star among them and was proud of his nick name, and had kept it all through his adult life.

Mole man lived in the hills that looked down at the petrol station. He had made a wooden hut under the trees, and was well hidden so far, he had seen no zombies up in the hills. He stood by a tree and saw the red van drive away from the petrol station.

"You will all die the hills are the only safe place to be," he shouted at the retreating tail gate of the red van. He had been in and out of prison all this life from the young offenders to the hard adult prisons. He didn't like it on the outside, and could never find work or the work he did find he hated and soon left. He only felt hate inside and so he would steal or fight and get himself in trouble so he could be someone in prison.

The outbreak had happened while he was out, and now he was glad if they had left him in a prison cell he would have starved to death. At first, he managed okay going from place to place, but the zombie's numbers were getting bigger, and then he had found the hills.

He had been here for around four or five months now and felt safe, and he was fine being alone he liked his own company.

==

Mole man went hunting cross bow in hand, and a small brown sack over his shoulder. He whistled to himself and saw the squirrel eating a nut or berry on a tree branch. He slowly took aim not making a sound and fired an arrow at the squirrel. His aim was true and the squirrel fell to the forest floor, he went over and put the squirrel in the brown sack.

"Maybe one more," he said to himself. The next one came along about half hour later and again his aim was true, and he smiled as he walked back with the two squirrels in his brown sack. He would eat well tonight.

He thought back to the young offender's prison that had been a good time after the tunnel incident. When he was extra hungry one of the boys would give him extra food when he needed a cigarette, they would get it for him. When another boy tried to pick on him, they would soon bring the boy down if he couldn't himself. Yes, life had been good in them days, and he was lost in thought as he walked into a zombie!

He was walking through a group of trees and bumped into the zombie, and the zombie went backwards. It was a girl with long dirty blonde hair her nose was missing, and she had dried blood all over her white dress.

"Holy fuck."

He was stunned it was the first zombie he had seen in the hills and forests. The zombie seemed to look at him, and then started to walk towards him its arms held out. Mole man aimed his cross bow and fired the arrow hit the zombie in the forehead, and it went down. He grabbed the arrow, and put his boot on its head and pulled it out.

"Mother fucker," he looked around him, but could see no more, but that didn't mean there wasn't.

"Shit."

Then he heard a twig snap close by and he thought he could hear moaning he headed back to his wooden hut quickly.

==

He was on his wooden cot, but he couldn't sleep he heard noises in the forest some close by then others far. Then it happened he heard something hit the wooden hut from the back! He was up in an instant he was already dressed what was the point of undressing for bed anyway.

He picked up his machete and went outside with a torch in his hand. The zombie was a fat man in trousers, and no top its belly hung over its belt. There was a gaping hole in its belly and scratches down its fat face. Mole man put the machete in the top of its head, and the fat zombie went down.

Two more zombies came out of the trees a young girl with a pink t-shirt and no eyes, her eyes were missing and mole man gasped! The other zombie was a man in a suit his face gone a shade of green the zombies were rotten, and the smell made him gag. He took a step forward, and sliced the top of the girls head off she collapsed to the ground.

Then four zombies came out of the trees, and he turned and another three came out from behind him. Mole man ran he left his belongings inside the wooden hut, and just ran.

The next morning, he came out on a river bank it was so peaceful it was hard to believe what had happened last night. He would have to go back and get his things, but he would wait for a little while.

The river was wide and he saw a boat travelling down the other side he waved his arms and jumped up and down.

"Hey hey help me," he shouted out.

But the boat carried on and did not stop. Mole man sighed and looked into the trees.

"Damn zombies I hate them."

He shrugged his shoulders and walked back into the trees no time like the present he would get his stuff, and move on again. At least it was day light and he would be able to handle the zombies better than at night. He thought to himself would he ever find a place that he could call home.

A real home that would be amazing but no the reality was that this was the world now and it was a survivor's world the weak would die. There was no place he could call home ever.

Chapter 6

Boat

Rick and Patty saw the man waving his arms on the river bank, but they didn't slow down, and they didn't look back.

"Maybe we should have stopped," Patty said pulling her curly brown hair out of her eyes it was a windy day on the river.

"No way he could have been a murderer for all we know," Rick replied looking at the river ahead.

Rick was forty-four and had short brown hair, and stubble on his cheeks and chin. He could never be called handsome his nose was too big and his chin jutted out, and he had beady little eyes. But Patty loved him and was looking forward to marrying Rick before the outbreak. She had a head of brown curly hair like a black chick from the seventies. She was a pretty black woman, and had a round kind face with a lovely smile.

There was a bang on the door and both looked towards the sleeping quarter's door which was locked. There good friend Vincent had been bitten before they found the boat, and when he died, they put him into the sleeping cabin.

"Shit, he has come back," Rick said looking at Patty.

"He is a zombie!"

"Damn it Patty don't use that word you know I hate it; he has come back."

"Please Rick just kill him we can't keep him like some pet."

Rick rubbed the stubble on his chin and sighed, "Your right honey."

The banging grew louder and then the moaning started.

"Shut him up Rick," Patty shouted putting her hands over her ears.

"Okay okay," he screamed back at her.

==

Rick had a hunting knife on his belt, and now held it tight in his hand he looked at Patty and smiled. She smiled back, but both smiles were strained.

"What are you going to do Rick."

"You open the door, and when it comes out, I will stab it."

"Okay but be careful you don't want a bite from a zombie."

"Stop calling it a zombie."

"He is dead Rick, and in my book, he is a zombie."

"No, he is one of the dead."

"Zombie," she liked to wind him up sometimes it was fun seeing his face go red.

"Don't say that word please."

"Oh, okay darling," she smiled at him and said, "Zombie," and laughed.

"Very funny Patty."

He coughed and looked at the cabin door and gripped the knife, "Okay Patty open the door."

Patty took the door knob in her hands and Rick couldn't help but look at her erect nipples through her tight top. Patty turned the door knob, and it clicked open she stood back and watched. Vincent stood in the door way as if he couldn't believe the barrier had been opened.

His once handsome face was now as white as marble, and he had dark shadows under his white eyes. Rick stood and raised the knife over his head as Vincent stumbled out its arms out stretched reaching for Rick. Rick plunged the knife down wards in an arc, and the blade went into the top of Vincent's head. The dead man fell face first, and hit the deck this time dead for good.

"Good job honey," Patty said clapping her hands.

"Thanks now give me a hand throwing him over the side he is starting to smell already."

The two of them picked up the body and with Patty on the legs rolled him over the side of the boat. The body hit the water with a splash, and they watched as the body began to slowly sink.

==

Rick saw the big old pub as the boat went round a bend in the river. The pub had a thatched roof, and wooden tables and benches on the outside. It looked abandoned and as they got closer, he could see some broken windows, but there had to be food inside.

"We need to investigate honey," he said to her.

"I'm not sure it looks spooky."

"Well, we need food."

Rick steered the boat over to the river bank next to a small jetty and jumped off, and tied up the boat.

"Come on honey," he said holding out his hand to her.

Patty took his hand and jumped off the boat. They walked up to the front of the pub the old rusted sign read *the badger.* There were empty beer glasses on some of the tables and some of the benches were tipped over as if people had made a quick exit. Rick pushed open the front door all was silent, and they moved inside.

The stale smell of beer hit them and something else mixed in with that as well, the smell of death! Rick saw the crisps and went over to the bar, the pub had a bar in the centre with bar stools all round. There was a dart board over to one side, and a pool table and an old duke box, and lots of tables and chairs. The black board sign told of the specials for that day, and a free pint of beer with all orders.

"Rick be quiet," Patty said as Rick stuffed bags of crisps into a plastic bag he had found on the floor.

Rick saw the basement door there could be barrels of beer down there he could murder a pint of beer. Plus, they could roll some over to the boat, and have a supply of beer the idea sounded good to him.

"Patty the cellar door open it and have a quick look."

She shrugged her shoulders, "Okay honey," she could see he was busy getting more crisps and peanuts. Patty walked over to the cellar door and took the knob in her hand she giggled as she thought I'm having a lot of knobs in my hand today.

She opened the door with not a care in the world, and looked into the darkness. Zombies poured out of the cellar! And she screamed as one an old woman grabbed her and took a chunk out of her shoulder. Blood ran down her arm as another zombie reached out for her, Patty stumbled back and ran for the front door, and not bothering to look back for Rick. Rick heard her scream, and then saw her running out of the pub, and then he saw the zombies!

There must have been thirty or forty of them, and he didn't stand a chance as some came behind the bar, and others blocked his way over the bar. He felt pain in his knee and looked down to see a dead boy with blonde hair biting into his knee.

He cried out and licked the dead boy in the head the boy went back only to be replaced by a huge fat bellied man in a cowboy hat. The dead cowboy took Rick in its arms and bit into his neck blood spurted out across the bar splattering the bottles of spirits on the optics.

Patty tripped and fell face first onto a table outside, panting and crying. She felt weak and walked over to the wall of the pub and slumped down with her back against it. She was so tired and closed her eyes.

"I've been bitten and now this is the end," she whispered.

Chapter 7

The group

The van stopped with the engine still running, and one of the windows went down. The man pocked his head out of the window and looked at *'the badger'* pub with some of its benches over turned and broken windows. He saw the dead black woman with the mass of curly brown hair which must have been dyed.

The van moved off and as it did so the black woman slumped against the badger's wall opened her eyes! Tony in the passenger seat turned to the driver John and said, "The pub was overrun by the dead I could see their shadows inside the pub."

Tony was a tall chubby man with a boyish face and short blonde hair he had a knife in his belt. John on the other hand was a fat short man with grey hair and a spotty chubby face with a grey goatee beard he had a hammer by his side.

"Yes, I saw them too mate that's why I drove off."

Both were touching fifty but Tony looked so much younger than his friend. In the back of the van sat Peter who held an axe in his hands he was a short thin man with glasses and short brown hair.

"Well, we need to find more food soon."

Hayden sat next to Peter he had a baseball bat by his side he was a big man with wide shoulders, and a bit of a belly, but this didn't take away the sear size of the man.

"Damn right on that one mate."

He was short but wide and next to him sat Julie the first of the two women in the group.

She was tiny and petit with long blonde hair and a pale white face with sharp features she held a knife, "I hate stopping those zombies freak me out."

Hayley completed the group she was also small with long dark hair and a pretty face, but her nose was far too big she held a crow bar, "Yes Julie me too."

==

The van stopped outside a house on a quiet street they were somewhere between Norwich and Ipswich.

"This will do for the night," Tony said to them all.

They climbed out of the van and John locked up with his key.

"Looks good to me I'm beat man," Hayden said looking at the old house. Peter and Hayden went round the back, and the others waited they didn't have to wait long as the two came back.

"It's good the back door was open, but no zombies," Hayden said to the group.

"But we will have to check the upstairs." Peter said. After ten minutes the group relaxed in the front room of the house, and Hayden and Peter used the sofa. There were two bedrooms upstairs bedrooms with beds and sheets the group would sleep well for once. Julie made coffee on the gas stove brought from the van, and they all ate spam or tuna from tins.

The group settled down for the night with John sleeping on the sofa in the front room. The two girls had a bed to themselves and Tony and Hayden had the bed and Peter a cot they found in the loft.

The next morning the group came down to the front room John was up and he looked at his friends and said, "Zombies!"

"Where," Tony asked.

"They are out the front and in the back garden," John replied.

"Must have been your bloody snoring John mate," Hayden said laughing.

Tony went to the front of the room and pulled back the curtains and looked out there were a few zombies in the front garden, but not too many they should be able to make it to the van no problem.

"Come on let's get back to the van," Tony said and they followed him into the hallway.

The front door opened and Tony led the way he hit one zombie across the face with his knife a long scar opened, and the zombie stumbled backwards. Tony looked at the fat zombie only wearing shorts with disgust, and moved on.

Hayden hit a woman zombie over the head with his baseball bat, and Hayley finished it off with the crow bar to the top of its head.

Peter brought up the rear and as he stepped over the still moving fat zombie on the ground, he felt pain rip up his right leg. The fat zombie with the shorts had bitten his leg, and now sat on the ground with a smug look on its fat face chewing his flesh.

"Fuck," Peter screamed and John turned and saw the blood on his leg.

"Oh, shit mate I'm so sorry," and with that John swung the hammer claw end and it embedded itself in the top of Peters head. John took the hammer out and blood spurted up out of the wound, and then Peter fell dead to the ground. The fat zombie crawled over to the still warm bloody, and began to feed John turned and ran to the van.

==

That afternoon the group found a super market in a small countryside village the super market had been raided on more than one occasion by the looks of it. The group dealt with the loss of Peter as best they could no one really wanted to talk about it John had done what was needed, and that was that. They all lived in a world now where death ruled the roost, and being upset could cost you your life you had to be on the ball at all times. Zombies didn't have feelings and they would take you down in a second given the chance. Hayden and Julie walked down one aisle it was a mess, and had a pool of blood on the floor, but so far, no zombies.

"Look a few cans," Julie said pointing and Hayden saw a tin can under the shelving. Hayden bent down and took the cans and held them up and laughed and looked at Julie and said, "We have marrow peas and carrots."

"Better than nothing."

"I guess your right Jules," and with that put them into his rucksack.

Hayley and John took the other aisles and didn't have much luck either they found two tins of chicken soup. They saw two dead decomposing bodies with flies swarming round them, and the smell man it was bad. They met Tony who had gone off on his own he had found some packets of cigarettes and chocolate bars.

"Come on guys let's get the fuck out of here," he said to them.

John drove the van and they travelled for many hours going down country lanes, and then he stopped the others were dozing off.

"Look Tony up ahead," John said pointing his finger at a sign in the road.

"Holy shit a dog rescue centre," Tony rubbed his smooth chin he never could grow any hairs on his chin or cheeks. Hayley popped her head out of the back and said, "An animal home what good is that."

"Might have food people do work there," Tony said with a sneer he thought Hayley a bit dense.

"Oh yes," she replied.

"Come on John drive in and let's have a look."

They checked the doors of the centre they were all locked.

"We will have to brake in," Hayden said waving his baseball bat in the air.

"No," John cried and then he went on, "I see an open back door through the dog pound."

Tony looked into the caged dog pound, and the bodies of several dogs over on the other side.

"Right, you and me John the rest wait here until we give the okay," Tony said he was unsure about those dog bodies.

"You sure them dogs are dead," Julie asked Tony. He nodded his head who the hell had ever heard of zombie dogs for fuck's sake. The cage was not pad locked and Tony slid the bolt across, and he and John entered the pound, and closed the door behind them. The others looked on as the two men walked silently across the tarmac heading towards the open-door way. Dog bowls on the ground all dried up there was no sign of any dog food, but the smell of death hung heavy in the air.

Tony stopped and looked at the bodies of the dead dogs had one of them moved. No surely not his eyes were playing tricks on him, and he smiled zombie dogs indeed. John also looked and then he screamed as the inside of the pound came to life!

It happened quickly one moment the dogs looked dead and then they came to life, and headed straight for the two men. The dogs had been resting and were half starved they had not been fed for days even feeding on the weaker dogs, and the noise had disturbed them now they got back on shaky legs and went for the two men. John ran but tripped over a dog bowl and Tony got tangled up in John's legs and fell on top of him. The skinny dogs you could see their ribs through lack of food closed in on the two men, and started to rip them apart with their sharp teeth.

Jack Russell's, a boxer dog with one leg missing a mongrel tearing out John's intestines so the small dogs could feed on these. Tony held his hand in the air the dogs going crazy with the welcome food, and then his hand dropped down among the furry mass. Hayden was sick on the ground, and Hayley grabbed his arm and pulled the big man.

"Come on let's get back to the van."

"What about John and Tony," he sobbed.

"They are dead now come on."

"God yes come on man," Julie cried.

==

The van ran out of petrol and Hayden sighed, and looked at the two girls in the front with him.

"Looks like we walk from here," he sighed again.

"Get all the stuff we need and put it in rucksacks," Hayley said and Julie moved into the back of the van.

They walked down a dark alley way that night with garden fences on both sides.

"I'm tired let's find a house to stay in for the night," Julie whined at them.

"Yes, okay Jules," Hayden said and began to climb over one of the wooden fences.

"Hey be careful Hayden," Hayley said with concern on her pretty face.

"Pot luck girls," he said with a laugh and then dropped down on the other side out of sight from the two girls.

They heard a chain rattle, and then Hayden cried out.

It was as dark as hell when Hayden dropped down onto the ground on the other side of the fence. The house was in darkness as was the garden then he heard a chain rattle close by, and then something grabbed him and he felt pressure on his neck, and then felt his flesh being ripped away.

"Run I've been bitten!" he screamed.

Blood ran down his shirt and trousers and he felt his legs go weak as the thing holding him took another bite out of him.

"Come on Julie it's over," Hayley said the group was finished.

"Oh my god what are we going to do," Julie sobbed.

"We survive that's what we do now come on," Hayley grabbed Julie's hand and began to run down the alley way going back the way they had come.

Chapter 8

Crazy

Danny Ross sat in his favourite chair and sighed he could hear some commotion from outside in the garden. He had the French windows open, and he would get up soon and have a look. He was a short man with a bald head and metal glasses; he had green eyes and a very pale face. Danny was fast approaching thirty-four, but he felt like he was ten years older since the zombie outbreak, but at least he still had his family. He lived in a three-bedroom house with two bathrooms one upstairs and one downstairs. The down stairs also had a kitchen and a living room, and the garden was big.

He had managed to keep his family together among all this madness.

His mother and father were chained up in the main bedroom together like they used to be those two were joined at the hip people would say. His mother Beverley had once been a pretty woman even in her late fifties his father Jack had been a tall man who ruled the roost. His sister Ruth was chained in the smaller room upstairs in her room of course. She was like a small doll with a white beautiful face with blue eyes, but they had gone dull now.

Danny had the other bedroom and it made him feel comfortable with his family so close by made him sleep well at night. His aunt Edna was chained in the kitchen, and she was making a noise now they did seem to sleep if nothing was going on or maybe they just went into silent mode.

You see all his family were zombies, but he had kept them all together his aunt Edna must have heard the noise from the garden as well. Danny got to his feet and walked out into the garden with a torch he walked down the brick pathway.

Both sides used to be full of flower beds, but he could not be bothered to keep them now that had been his mother's job. There good friend and neighbour was chained at the bottom of the garden near the shed, and he must have made the noise. Danny shone the light and saw the large man on the ground he was dead of course his neighbour had seen to that. He could see the bloody wound on the man's throat.

The zombie looked into the light as it munched on a large piece of the man's flesh, and growled at Danny.

"Less of that Arthur you just be quiet, and enjoy your meal."

==

Danny came in from the garden and closed the French windows and locked them he was feeling tired now. He didn't know what time it was he had given up on that when the power went down, and every bloody clock in the house was electric. They couldn't be like normal people and have battery operated clocks oh no.

He sat down on the sofa and laid his head back he would nap on the sofa for a while. He looked at the dark hole that was the open kitchen doorway, and smiled at least he had his aunt

Edna close by that made him feel good, and he closed his eyes.

Danny was chained to a brick wall he could see the wall on both sides and it went on forever he couldn't see an end to the wall. He looked up but could only see a dark sky with no clouds, but he could make out shapes. Things that screamed and flew with large wings they looked like dragons, and they breathed fire too. He cried out as pain hit his stomach, he was so hungry, and he bent down as far as the chains would let him.

His eyes filled with tears how could he be so hungry.

Then he looked in front of him and he could see humans he knew they were humans because he could smell them. Then he saw his hands in the chains rotting hands with the flesh peeling off in strips!

They were laughing at him and pointing then they drew closer, but not to close and he went wild with the smell of their flesh, and it was making the hunger grow worse. His sister Ruth pointed at him she was lovely, and looked young with her sparkling blue eyes.

"Is Danny hungry," she laughed at him.

Then his mother came close she looked wonderful and had her red hair tied back in a pony tail it was how he remembered them all.

"My poor boy Danny," she said with a smile.

His father came up to him tall and fall of pride.

"You idiot how could you have got bitten," he said sadly.

Aunt Edna came to him with her walking stick waving at him.

"It's your own fault young man," she hissed at him. Then Arthur appeared but he was still a zombie, and he offered Danny the arm of the big guy from the garden.

Then sudden pain in his arm had the humans bitten him then he was awake, and he screamed as pain shot up his arm! Somehow Aunt Edna had gotten out of her chains, and was now chewing on the flesh of his arm.

Blood ran down his arm and pooled on the sofa.

==

Danny clamed himself down and took hold of his Aunt Edna around the neck and frog marched her back into the kitchen. She was an old fragile zombie, and he easily put the chain back on her some of the chain had snapped, but he clipped the catch on to unbroken part.

"There you go Auntie," he said as the zombie tired to get at him once more.

"Now you calm down you have eaten already."

He went upstairs and into the bathroom he could hear moaning from the other bedrooms the noise must have woken them all. He bathed the wound in stale water he had a bath tub of it, and put a bandage round the arm, but he knew it was only a matter of time now. He went across the landing and into his bedroom he lay down and closed his eyes.

He was a soldier in the second world war and he was in a muddy trench with a rifle pointing out into no man's land. He saw dark shapes moving slowly, and began to fire at them, but they seemed to be indestructible and kept coming. He could hear his comrades screaming and shouting, and running through the trench like headless chickens. A young man with a handsome face that had had never seen a razor yet clapped him on the back and screamed.

"Come on man move let's get out of there they are coming!"

Then he was gone and Danny was alone in the trench with the moaning shapes now closer. He started to fire at them then stopped as the army of zombies piled into his trench, and he screamed as dead bodies fell on top of him.

He woke up from the dream he was sweating badly the fever of the dead had taken hold of him there was not much time left.

==

He staggered down the stairs holding onto the stair rail he felt like just giving up and falling, but he had to keep going. He heard his Aunt Edna as he passed the kitchen it was light outside now as he opened the French windows. He staggered down the pathway, and paused to get his breath at the shed. Arthur looked at him with his dead eyes, and moaned rattling his chain the big guy had gone.

There were blood stains on the ground but no body Danny looked around, and saw the fence separating their garden from the neighbours had been broken. The big guy must have smashed his way out oh well too late to catch up with him now, and make him one of the family. He went into the shed and picked up a chain and a padlock. Back upstairs in his bedroom Danny chained himself to his bed and laid down for the last time the fever was burning up his whole body.

Not much time left in his world.

"Now I can be with my family," he said in a whisper and closed his eyes.

Chapter 9

Hunter

The tall thin man entered the garden of the house and went straight to the French windows. It was getting late, and he needed somewhere to hole up for the night he heard the sound of a chain in the garden, but ignored it. He put his elbow through the thin glass, and opened the French windows then locked them behind him. He was an Indian man tall and thin like a skeleton with a bald head and hard dark eyes. He had scars on both cheeks from a village growing up ceremony done in his youth.

He had a mean looking face and felt very little emotion it was the way he had been brought up in the small village in the hills of Latur India. He had come to England five years ago to help his uncle with his corner shop. It had been a good arrangement no one stole from the shop with the tall mean looking guy watching over them.

Then the outbreak had happened and the world had gone to shit, but it didn't bother him as long as he survived on his own. He was an expert with a cross bow which he held in his hand, and had two large hunting knives in his belt around his thin waist. Hunter he was by nature and by name, he moved into the house, and stopped he heard moaning from the kitchen. He entered the kitchen and saw the old woman zombie straining at the chain. Hunter took aim and shot the zombie dead centre in the forehead the old dead woman dropped to the floor now still.

He moved upstairs and dealt with the two people chained to the master bed, and then the young girl in the smaller room. He sat on the final bed and looked at the dead man and took the arrow out of its head. What crazy fucker had done this must have been as mad as a hatter.

He looked at the final corpse not as old as the others he guessed that this man had chained his family up, and had somehow got bitten himself so decided to join them. Hunter nodded his head yes that sounded about right he didn't like unsolved puzzles. He took some clean sheets out of a cupboard in the man's bedroom, and made a bed in the bath tub after clearing the water. He slept like a baby in the bath tub, and didn't wake until the next morning.

==

Hunter found some soup cans and ate one of them and put two into a rucksack he found in the girl's room. It was plain brown colour and suit him well he had not even thought of carry a rucksack he just ate as he went, but it would come in handy for sure. He went out of the French windows and heard the chain again, and he saw the man chained up by the shed.

The man who had done all this really was crazy; Hunter shot the man zombie in the head, and moved on over the garden fence. He saw a large man zombie in another garden just walking up and down as if it were lost and trying to find a way out. Blood covered his front, and the open wound on its throat had a swarm of flies around it.

Hunter left the roaming zombie and carried on.

He hit the country lanes that afternoon the country side would be good he was sick of all the overrun cities and towns. As he rounded a corner, he saw two zombies shambling towards him on the road, he stopped and let them catch up with him. One zombie wore a policeman's uniform, and had part of his cheek missing, it was a large fat zombie, and also had part of its belly missing intestines were dragging along the road after it. The other zombie was a naked woman her small breasts looked green now, and her shaved pussy dried and had sores all over it and her belly.

They were decaying badly and Hunter wasted no time in shooting both in the head. He retrieved his arrows and gave them a good wipe. He saw an old shed close to a farm and made his way over to it. All was clear and he went inside there was dried straw, and he made his bed and soon fell into a deep sleep.

He woke up suddenly and saw two people standing over him.

"Make one move you black motherfucker and I will kill you."

==

"I'm Bradford and this is Sue, and you my friend are in deep shit," the man laughed after introducing himself and his partner. Hunter was tied up inside the shed the man Bradford was a fat man with an old looking face his hair receding badly and fat cheeks that wobbled when he spoke.

"I'm Hunter and I mean you both no harm just let me be on my way."

But he knew he had no chance the woman was small and petite with long dark hair, but her face was spotty and she looked old.

"We don't give a shit about you mate," Sue hissed at him.

"He might come in handy with the zombies," Bradford laughed. Yes, these two were bandits because that's what they had to be, roaming the towns robbing and looting. Answering to no one and using others for their gain they would throw Hunter to the zombies if it would save their lives.

"Get up you black bastard," Bradford said and grabbed Hunters arm and pulled him up.

"We are going for a little walk through the forest," the fat man added.

"Yes, and you are bait if we run into any zombies," Sue said with a smile.

"Damn right baby," Bradford said clapping his hands.

==

Hunter was truly getting pissed off the fat man Bradford kept shoving him in the back.

"Come on move it," Bradford would say after every shove. Hunter spied a group of zombies close by, but the two bandits had not noticed them. The rope that bound his hands was loose now, and he could easily escape, but he had to time it just right. Hunter saw the small ditch by some bushes and walked towards it the other two didn't notice the slight change in direction. Hunter fell into the ditch the zombies were now really close, and he cried out as well to get their attention.

"Hey what the fuck," Bradford said as the black man disappeared into a ditch.

"I didn't see it," Hunter lied.

"Oh my god," Sue said as the group of zombies came at them!

Hunter had his hands free and was up on his feet quickly he hit Bradford square on the jaw, and the fat man went down on his backside.

"You black cunt," Bradford said rubbing his jaw on the dirty ground. Hunter kicked him in the head, and Bradford went down hard on his back. Hunter grabbed Sue and pushed her to the ground he got his two knifes off her, and his cross bow.

"I will have these back bitch," he hissed at her. The group of zombies zeroed in on Bradford and sank down on their knees and started to tear him apart. Hunter grabbed Sue and pushed her up and forwards.

"Move it bitch unless you want to be zombie meat."

Hunter looked back and saw one zombie chewing on Bradford's arm another zombie had pulled off a leg, and was sitting against a tree trunk eating.

Bradford lay in a pool of blood and the group of zombies feed well and Hunter smiled. More zombies pulled out the man's steaming intestines, and hungrily bit into them.

==

Hunter found another old barn later that day and shoved Sue into it hard she fell onto the ground sobbing. Hunter closed the door and tied Sues hands up behind her back.

"Now how does it feel bitch."

"Please please don't hurt me," she pleaded with him. He should rape her and torture her, but he really couldn't be bothered, and besides she was not his type.

"Don't worry bitch I am not going to do anything to you."

"Why did you hang around with that creep," Hunter asked

"I used to work with him before all this started and it just seemed like a good idea," Sue sobbed.

Hunter shook his head and said, "If humans are ever going to get over this we must work together."

But he knew his words meant nothing the world was finished. Sue sobbed until she fell asleep Hunter was thinking too much lately, and he struggled to sleep, but went off eventually.

Next morning, they were walking across a field Hunter could see a group of zombies on the other side, and headed that way.

"Hey there are zombies over there," Sue said with fear in her voice there was nothing worse than being tied up with hungry zombies baring down on you.

"I can see that bitch."

Hunter had decided last night that he needed to get rid of the ugly looking bitch. As they got closer Hunter took out one of his hunting knifes, he went up to the back of Sue, and stabbed her in the back. She gasped and fell to her knees the breath pushed out of her body.

He had stabbed her not to kill her, but to only paralyse her legs he calmly walked away as the zombies came to at the prone woman.

"Better this way," he smiled as he walked onwards on his own again.

==

Hunter came into a clearing and heard a scream he raced towards the sound, and saw an old farm house. It was a white bungalow with a thatched roof and there were zombies going through the open front door. He raced over and started to shoot the zombies in the head one was fresh, and as the arrow hit it in the back of the head blood burst from the wound. Two of the zombies were kids, but Hunter did not hesitate and took them both out. The zombie girl with the pink dress looked sweet even in death as Hunter moved into the farm house.

He saw an old woman with white hair holding a boy of about fifteen, and crying.

The woman was Biddy she had white hair and was plump with large breasts she was Irish and had a sweet smile, and came across as a good woman. The boy was Clive and was her grandson he was short and weedy looking.

She made tea and Hunter drank gratefully.

"Poor Clive saw his dad and opened the front door," Biddy said rubbing the boy's hair and smiling.

"Lucky I was around," Hunter said sipping his hot tea she had an old wood oven.

"Look Hunter we have a car outside loaded with supplies come with us."

She had told him about how all of their family were dead, and the farm house was just not safe anymore.

Hunter shook his head no, "I'm sorry Biddy but I have to be alone."

"Why do you have to be alone," the boy asked him and Hunter smiled at the boy.

"Because Clive people die when they are around me."

Chapter 10

Car jack

Biddy put the car in gear it was an old beat-up blue Nissan sunny, but it still ran from A to B. She watched Hunter in the mirror, and saw him move off waving to them as he went. Hunter watched the old car move off he could sense the old woman looking at him, and he saw the small boy wave at him. He waved back and then turned and moved off wishing the two luck on their journey.

Biddy drove through the countryside and Clive sat in the back with the bags of supplies around him in supermarket carrier bags. They had crisps, tins of soup and meat and fish plus bottles of water and coke. They would be okay for a while before they would have to find more supplies. Top of the list for Biddy was finding a safe place to stay they couldn't keep driving around, and then there was the problem of finding petrol.

Clive watched the countryside rush past, and thought about his mother and father. They worked in the city and they never came home to the farm after the outbreak. The boy remembered watching the television and hoping to see his parents, there were a lot of reports at first from London. But of course, the television went dead like most of the people as the zombies grew in numbers.

His grandmother Biddy had tried her best to take the pain away, but Clive hoped his parents were alive somewhere maybe holed up from the zombies. When he was bigger, he would go to London, and find them in his young mind he was sure of that.

==

That night Biddy pulled over to the side of a country lane, and turned off the car engine.

"Let's get something to eat, and then try and get some sleep."

"Yes Gran."

"You're a good brave boy," she said smiling and running a hand through his hair.

"When will the zombies go Gran?"

She looked at the small boy in the dying light and sighed, "Soon I hope."

She knew it was a lie, but she had to make the boy believe they had hope. They ate a tin of tuna each and a bag of crisps, and Biddy had water, Clive some coke. Clive closed his eyes and imagined he was all grown up. He was running in the centre of London, and he had a machine gun in his hands and he was cutting zombies in half as he fired at them. He was fearless and enjoyed killing the zombies, they could not touch him in his mind. Then he came to a boarded-up shop, and called out, he knew his parents were inside. Then the boards were ripped down and the door opened, and out came his parents.

"Good night, Clive sweet dreams and sleep well."

The spell of the day dream was finished and he yawned, "Good night, Gran."

==

They had only been driving for half an hour when Biddy turned a corner of a small country lane, and almost ran into a road block!

"Holy shit," she cried out as she put the brakes on.

"What Gran," Clive said startled from the back. There were two cars parked across the road, and four men in army uniforms they were holding guns. One of the men walked towards the car he looked big like he done body building.

"Oh, thank god they will help us Clive."

"Great Gran," but young Clive was scared he didn't like the look of the men. Biddy got out of the car and faced the large man he was of medium height, but very wide. He smiled at her and she saw that he was bald; he had a chubby face with stubble on his chin.

"Oh, thank god we found you sir."

The man let out a deep laugh, and then said in a cold voice, "Yes it's your lucky day."

Another army man walked behind Biddy she saw him as he went past the car. He was an ugly man and looked cross eyed; he had dark hair and an evil smile. The man behind her grabbed her breasts she gasped in fear.

"Come on mate lets all fuck her she is old but she's got damned nice tits."

"Leave her alone, and throw her back in the car we are not killers or rapists yet," said the bald man. The ugly man pushed her back into the car he then went round the back and took out all of the supermarket carrier bags.

"Damn man they got loads of food here."

"Good then put it in our car," then the bald man walked round the Nissan sunny and took out a hand gun, and proceeded to blow out all four tires. Biddy was sobbing in the front they had no food and now no car. The bald man tapped on the window screen and smiled.

"You have a nice day now Madame."

And with that he walked off all four men climbed into one of the cars it was a people carrier, and drove off.

As the night drew in Biddy saw the dark shadows among the trees nearby. Then she saw the zombies across the road!

She made sure all the doors were locked and climbed into the back with Clive.

"Now Clive stay still and don't say a word, and they will go away okay."

"Okay Gran."

The first zombie banged on the car door then another started hitting the window screen. Biddy hugged Clive and tears ran down her cheeks. How could things have gone wrong so quickly, now she had no chance of saving the boy?

Clive was her world and she would protect him with her last breath, but she didn't fancy their chances much now. All she had was God and Jesus Christ to believe in, and she began to pray in her mind.

Chapter 11

The army men

The four former army men were silent as they rode in the van; they had stolen the van a short while after leaving the old woman and the boy. Driving two cars had been too much of a pain it was better to travel in a group, and they had spotted the white van in someone's drive. Of course, they had taken the van finding the keys inside the house along with some valuable cans of food, and thankfully no zombies.

George sat in the passenger seat he had a bald head and was a well-built young man at twenty-four. He was training to be a mechanic and electrician in the services he was also interested in plumbing and building before the outbreak had put all of that on hold.

Stephen was driving he was a fat ugly man, and sneered at most things. He hated people and wished they had raped the old woman with the big tits damn he hadn't had a woman for ages now. He was thirty and had a fat piggy face with a beard he couldn't be bothered to shave in fact he couldn't be bothered to do a lot of things he was lazy.

Glenn was in charge being the highest rank and sat in the back he was thirty-five, and had always been in the army. He had funny eyes that made him look boss eyed, but he was a jolly man and liked to joke around. He had thick dark hair and was unshaven he wasn't a good-looking man, but seemed to attract women and was never short before the outbreak.

Randall sat with Glenn in the back of the van he was twenty-one with brown hair cut short. He was a good-looking man and loved to flirt with the girls he also loved playing football and was good. In his youth he had trails with a Crystal Palace a top flight football team, but ended up playing for non-league Carshalton Athletic.

They had been on the road since the zombie out break the army base having been overrun by the living dead. They had hit the road with the two cars, and driven from town to town. They met some people, but took no one in with them and would often just rob the people, and leave them stranded just like the old woman and the kid. They would take no prisoners and fools would be dealt with by a bullet to the head.

==

"Hey look at that guys," they had been driving for hours and as the sun went down and the darkness took over Stephen spotted a light coming from a house.

"What is it?" Glenn said from the back.

"Just seen some lights on in a house boss," George said from up front.

"Right, everyone out," Glenn said looking at Randall as the van stopped.

"Yes sir," Randall replied getting out of the van quickly.

"Okay I want Stephen and George to investigate," Glenn said to the two holding rifles.

"Okay sir action at last," Stephen sneered.

"Be careful and no noise I just want you to report back what you see okay," Glenn looked from one to the other.

"Yes, sir don't worry," George said and the two men moved off.

"You want a cigarette boss," Randall offered to Glenn who took one as he watched his two men move off into the darkness towards the house in the countryside.

Stephen reached the side of the farm house a small white bungalow.

"Hey see anything yet," George asked close behind him.

"I am going to move by the window you stay close behind me."

"Okay mate," George replied.

Stephen looked through a gap in the boarded-up window he saw three people sitting on the floor a gas burner cooking some food on the floor. He could make out a woman and a man and a younger man. He could see no weapons at all and smiled this would be just too easy, but at least they had a place for the night, and maybe some pussy as well.

The night was cold and Glenn rubbed his hands together as Stephen and George came back.

"Easy pickings boss two men and a woman no weapons and they have a small gas cooker," Stephen sneered.

"The place is boarded up and looks secure sir," George added. Glenn sighed and went into deep thought he was fed up of sleeping in cars and vans.

"Sounds like a good idea boss I'm fed up of sleeping in vehicles," Randall said scratching his handsome face.

"Yes, we could all do with a good night's sleep," Glenn said smiling and then added, "But I don't want any killing okay," he said looking at all of them in the dark.

They nodded, and Stephen just gave an ugly sneer.

Clinton Reed was forty-five with receding grey hair and a wrinkled face he looked so much older than his actual age. He looked at his wife Cindy with her short red hair, she was still a good-looking woman at forty-one. Then there was Ian their twenty-year-old son who had long brown hair tied back in a pony tail. He had a bushy beard on a handsome face he was skinny like his father. They had been on the move since the outbreak staying away from the cities, and keeping to the countryside.

They had found this house two weeks ago, and had stayed in it ever since. Zombies rarely came this way, and when they did, they didn't seem to stay around for long. The answer to survival was to stay quiet, and just let the dead walk on by. They planned to stay in the bungalow for some time when they needed supplies they would venture into the nearest town.

There were two bedrooms with beds and covers, and the family slept well. The kitchen wasn't used and the bathroom was kept locked the smell was just horrible. They just spent their time in living room and bed rooms they done their toilet outside in a hole by the trees in the garden. Each looking out for who ever needed to go they had baseball bats, and an axe for weapons. Yes, the family were doing okay, and they liked the place which kept them safe from the dead.

==

Glenn led the soldiers to the small white bungalow, and he waited to the side of the door with Stephen and Randall on the other side. They had decided that George would knock on door, and plead with the family to let him in. George drew back his hand and knocked hard on the front door.

"Help me please help me," He shouted out.

They could hear footsteps on the other side of the door then a man's voice.

"Who the hell is that?"

"Please help me the zombies are close please let me in."

"Go away."

Then they heard a woman's voice, "Clinton for god's sake let them in."

They heard the bolt being drawn back, and then the light spilled out as the front door opened. The soldiers pushed their way inside Stephen holding a gun to the man's head. The woman put her hand to her mouth as Randall let off a round of bullets just outside the front door.

"Quit that you will attract the zombies you fool," cursed Glenn.

The four soldiers held the family guard and they sat down the gas cooker cooking what smelled like soup. Two strong oil lanterns burned on either side of the room the light they let off was good.

"Okay No noise and no trouble," Glenn said to the scared family.

"Look we are all in this together why take us prisoners," Clinton asked the man.

"I said shut up didn't I," Glenn pointed his rifle at the man.

"Now who are you anyway?"

"I am Clinton and this is my wife Cindy and our boy Ian."

"Okay good now listen Clinton I want your wife to cook extra soup then we talk."

Stephen finished his soup he was tired of talking he wanted the woman she looked okay for an older bitch, and had nice tits.

"Look Clinton, we won't harm you we are just looking for a place to stay the night then we move on."

Clinton nodded his head and smiled.

"Fuck this Glenn I want the woman," Stephen said getting to his feet, and pointing his hand gun at the woman.

"Yes, he has a point," Randall said he was feeling horny too. Glenn looked at his two soldiers they were under a lot of stress, and he knew a woman could relieve some of that he couldn't denial them this.

"Okay Stephen take the bitch into the bedroom."

Clinton looked at Glenn his eye brows raised, "Hey you said you weren't going to harm us."

Glenn shrugged, "Sorry mate I lied."

Stephen took the woman Cindy roughly, and pushed her into the dark bedroom.

"You struggle bitch and I will give you a mouth full," Stephen said then he was gone.

"You fucking pig," the woman screamed.

"Hurry up mate I'm horny too you know," Randall called to him. George just sat in a corner watching the scene play out he had no interest in the woman. He could hear the dead outside the sound of the shooting must have drawn them to the cottage.

==

There were no sounds coming from the bedroom, and Glenn moved closer and listened then Stephen emerged from the dark.

"Where is the woman?" Glenn asked.

Stephen sneered and shrugged, "She struggled so I killed the whore."

Clinton was on his feet and going towards Stephen.

"You bastard," he shouted then the banging started on the boards of the windows as the zombies could hear the commotion going on. Randall grabbed Clinton round the throat and pulled him backwards both men went back hard, and Randall's back hit the boarded-up window.

The boards cracked and then Randall screamed as hands from outside grabbed at his body, and he let go of Clinton. They watched in stunned silence as Randall was pulled through the broken window screaming as he went, then they heard eating noises amidst the screaming.

"Get these fuckers off me," Randall screamed then went silent. Zombies started to climb through the window, and Stephen and Glenn started to fire at them. A big fat zombie which was bare chested took a bullet in the chest, and then the head it fell to the floor another skinny zombie with no nose fell over the big zombie's body. George was stunned into action from the corner of the room, and shot the skinny zombie in the head as it crawled towards him. He could see the ruined nose and the cartilage bone showing through the zombie's nose, and it make him feel sick. Glenn pointed the rifle at Clinton, and cried out at the man, "You cunt you killed Randall."

Clinton held up his hands, "Not me the zombies pal."

Glenn shot the man in the head the boy Ian cried out, and raced to his dead dad's side.

"No dad."

"Everyone out now move it," shouted Glenn. The three soldiers left the sobbing boy, and raced out of the front door leaving it wide open.

"What about the boy," George asked as they raced outside.

"Fuck him," Stephen cried out shooting a girl zombie in the head she was wearing a summer frock. They made it back to the van and piled in. Stephen started the engine, and they roared off into the night.

==

"I need a shit," Stephen said and pulled the van over near a group of trees.

"Well hurry the fuck up," Glenn said the cottage incident had unnerved him a bit.

"Fuck man Randall's dead," George said from the back of the van. Stephen left the van and moved towards the trees. All seemed to be quiet and he pulled down his trousers, and squatted down. He thought back to the woman at the cottage she had been a fucking whore. He had taken out his penis and told her to suck it, she had told him to go to hell, and that she would bite the little thing off. Then she said that she had seen a bigger penis on a new born baby, and Stephen had seen red and he hit her hard. Then he had just taken her head in his arms and broken her neck.

"Fucking whore," he cursed into the darkness as he began to shit.

A dirty green hand one of its fingers missing grabbed a tuff of his short hair and pulled; he lost his balance and fell his legs landing in his own fresh shit.

He screamed as another zombie came at him from the front!

He felt a chunk of his cheek being torn away, and then the zombie in front was on top of him, and the smell that hit his nose was awful. He screamed again as the zombie in front bit into his exposed throat blood pumped out of the wound, and two more zombies joined in the feast. Glenn started the engine and moved off both men had heard the screams, and they were the screams of a dying man.

"What about Stephen," sobbed George from the back.

"Stephen is dead," Glenn almost shouted.

==

Glenn saw the farm house and pulled into the small lane that was lined with bushes. Then they came out into a clearing and the farm house stood there looking abandoned. He stopped the van and got out it had started to rain, and he heard the back door of the van open. He thought he heard the trees and under growth rustling nearby, and wanted to be inside quickly.

"Why we stopped here," asked George looking at the farm house.

"Because we need somewhere to hole up for a while, I'm fed up of travelling around."

Glenn was truly fed up, and now two of his men were dead in the matter of hours.

"Come on." Glenn said and George followed him. Glenn kicked in the locked front door and they moved into the darkness. Then a light came on and they starred at the large farmer, and his two young daughters well they assumed they were his daughters.

"What the fuck do you want?" Said the big man with a pitch fork in his hands.

He was a fearsome sight muscles bulged out of his shirt, and the light shined on his bald head. The two girls must have been fourteen or fifteen one had blonde hair the other brown.

"We just want somewhere to stay the night," Glenn said pointing his gun at the large man. George looked at the girls, and eyed them up and down. The farmer saw the sexual lust in the soldier's eyes, and knew if he let these men stay, they would rape his daughters for sure.

"Look if its supplies you want, I have loads in the basement,"

Glenn laughed what the hell was a farmer going to do against guns, "Yes good idea we will fill our van up with your supplies then we will have a bit of fun I think."

"Damn right," George said licking his lips the girls were young but stunning.

"I'm Jason and these are my daughters Tina and Gina."

"Oh, very original names who is who."

"Never you mind I will show you the basement," he said looking at his girls.

"Okay George you go to the basement I will cover the girls," Glenn said smiling at the two girls.

"Okay boss."

George followed the large farmer down the corridor, and they came to a locked door.

==

Jason stopped by the basement door with a large smile on his face these bastards would get what they deserved. George held his rifle out towards the large farmer, and saw the smile on his face.

"Why are you so happy?"

His smile dropped and he looked hard at the young soldier who was soon to die, "I have to smile young man to keep from going insane in this mad fucked up world."

George nodded his head damn right to that he thought. Jason used to have a large family and they were all close by, when the outbreak had happened, they had stayed together, but soon the group became just three. Some were bitten and changed some were old and died, but the one thing Jason couldn't do was kill them a second time he liked his family close. Jason opened the door and steeped back as a horde of zombies came out and attacked George!

George stood there as the door was opened, and the big farmer stepped to the side he looked into the gloom, and then saw the dead rush out at him, and he screamed! He didn't have time to fire his weapon as the zombies took him and he fell backwards onto the floor. A zombie with grey hair and a cooking apron on bit into his neck, another grabbed his arm, and took two of his fingers off, blood sprayed in an arc. Another zombie wearing a baseball shirt was sprayed with blood as it fell to its knees in front of the dying soldier eager to taste the flesh.

Jason moved quickly into the living room and shouted out, "The zombies have got in you must have left the fucking front door open."

Glenn raced into the hallway and Jason moved the girls out of the French windows. There were only two slow zombies outside, and Jason and the girls reached the pickup truck it was already loaded with supplies in case of emergencies like now. Glenn heard the truck start up and just stood watching the zombies eat his dead friend his blood must have still been warm.

Glenn moved out of the house the front door had been locked the crazy farmer must have kept the dead in the basement. He stood in the front of the house on the gravel, and looked at his van then his head exploded in a spray of blood and brains!

Jason smiled as he took the shot with the rifle the bastard got what he deserved.

He drove off quickly away from his home heading to God knew where.

Chapter twelve

Cats

Paul Hard stopped walking through the trees as he heard the pickup truck roar by on the country lane. He raced onto the tarmac of the lane, but the truck was racing off into the distance as it had roared by, he had seen a big man with a bald head at the wheel, and two young girls.

"Fuck it," he cursed, but keeping his voice low he didn't want zombies to know his location.

Paul was thirty and was going bald his grey hair now just went around the sides of his head. He had brown eyes and wore glasses he was as blind as a bat without them. He was a tall man at well over six foot three, and he was skinny with it. His last girlfriend had laughed at him when he had taken off his shirt actually laughed, and said he had an in growing chest. It was true his chest did go inwards rather than outwards.

He had lived in the city of Ipswich then the outbreak had happened. He didn't know what happened to his girlfriend because he left her, and Ipswich behind as he made for the countryside. He was heading for his nanny's place he loved his nanny so much and missed her; since his parents had died, he thought more and more about her.

So, the first thing that came to mind when the world started to fall apart was go to nannies. His nanny lived alone in a small country cottage she had white hair always tied into a bob. She was a plump old girl, but always with a smile and a good word.

The one thing she loved just as much as Paul was her cats, she had about twenty of the things. She knew Paul didn't like them, and she would keep them locked in the spare room when he visited her. Paul carried on walking towards his nans small town it wasn't too far now, he had been on the road for weeks now.

==

Paul sat down and rested his back on a tree trunk he was tired now, and it had started to rain. He had spied a small hut like thing in the middle of a field must be some kind of shed he had to get up, and reach it or he would be soaked the sky had become black. He walked to the hut and found it was a small storage shed he went inside, and closed the door there was no lock. There were tools and bottles holding liquids the shed was made of corrugated metal sheets.

It kept the rain off him and he sat down on the wooden boards used as a floor. The rain pounded down now and he could barely hear himself think. He closed his eyes he was so tired.

==

He woke up suddenly he had heard a noise from outside the hut, but the inside of the hut had changed. The tools and bottles had gone, and there was nothing but straw inside the hut. There was no door and he could make out something big in the darkness. The moon shone down suddenly the clouds moving off, and he saw a large shape watching him. Then the smell hit him it smelt like a pig sty, and then he realized the shape was in fact a pig.

It was joined by another pig and then another soon they were making a terrible squealing noise, and he put his hands over his ears. Then the pigs came into the hut and grabbed his legs and pulled him out he screamed!

His mind told him that a group of pigs could eat a man within a few minutes. He screamed as the pigs came at him squealing in what sounded like delight at the meal before them. Paul woke up in a sweat, and then heard the noise from outside.

==

There was a moaning noise and Paul knew it was a zombie hopefully just one. The door had no lock and Paul moved to the door and held it tight the moaning grew louder, and the thing was now on the other side of the door. Paul cursed the day light was starting to push away the night now. He saw the axe hanging along one wall and let the door go, and reached for the axe. The door opened and into the hut came a small zombie it was a boy with dirty blonde hair.

The boy wore a school uniform and his cheeks had been chewed away and one arm was missing. The zombie boy snarled at him and Paul swung the axe, the boys head came off easily and hit the far wall of the hut. Paul was sick in a corner.

"Fucking zombies."

He walked out of the hut and saw three more zombies walking towards the hut he made his way in the opposite direction still holding the axe.

==

He walked towards the small town and thought about his incidents with the living dead. He had been lucky in the fact that he had pretty much stayed out of their way so far. The boy had been the first he had killed or killed a second time more like. He had run into a pretty girl zombie as he left the city, he had stopped for a second, and looked at her pretty face. Her white eyes starred at him she had blood on her dress, but apart from that she looked almost normal. He had pushed her out of the way, and ran onwards.

He had heard them and seen them in the woods, but had managed to stay clear of them he had no weapon back then anyway. He would go to his nans she would look after him and together they could out ride this until help arrived and the world went back to normal. He stepped onto the main road of the town just as the light began to fade once more, he was excited not far now only just down the road.

==

He kept behind the tree and saw the house was in darkness that was odd she would have kept a light on. The zombies couldn't have gotten in surely his Nan was an intelligent woman, but she was old now as well he hoped she was okay. He could put up with the cats for her sake, and the sake of survival. He moved to the house and went along the wall to the back of the house it was a white bungalow. The front door he had seen was firmly shut, but the back door was open.

"Shit," he hissed quietly. He moved towards the door and looked inside all was quiet. Then in the gloom he saw one of the cats moving slowly towards him, as it drew nearer it hissed at him, but it sounded like there was no air behind the hiss, like a dry hiss it was hard to describe.

The cat went up his leg and Paul grabbed the thing and held it at arm's length the bloody thing stank, and it was a zombie. He threw the cat hard at the wall, and a wet bloody patch stayed on the wall as the cat slumped to the floor.

"Fucking cats are zombies too."

He moved inside and closed the back door.

He looked out of the large windows in the back room, and saw his Nan in the back garden he had missed her because she was out by the fish pond. She was dead, and he sobbed at the sight of her moving aimlessly around. There came a sound from the living room, and Paul moved off to investigate.

He opened the door and stepped into the dark living room he was looking forward to going into the bed room and have a sleep on a real bed. The sound intensified as he entered, and he realized he was surrounded by cats. Zombie cats and Paul screamed as the cats came at him, and soon his body was under a furry mass!

His nan ambled in some time later as if to see what her beloved cats were up to. Then Paul stood before her his face in shreds from the cat claws. The two zombies sat down on the sofa, and the zombie cats joined them.

Chapter thirteen

Clowns

The two people came out of the woods, and paused and stayed hidden as they watched two zombies go passed them. The man zombie was horrible, its face was chewed up just a red mask, and its clothes so tattered and ripped apart like some beast had gotten hold of him. Then they saw the dead cats following the two things that had once been human, and Barry nearly gasped, but managed to keep his mouth shut.

The mangled zombies and its cat pals went into the distance and Barry and Chloe came out onto the road way. They had been keeping to the countryside, and now they were near the motorway which they would follow. Barry was a tall thin man with black messy hair and a long beak of a nose. His companion was a small woman with long dark hair, and green eyes set in a delicate face.

Barry had been on his own when the outbreak occurred, he was a plumber by trade, and was out riding to a job when he saw his first zombie. He had listened to the radio, and had laughed at the idea of dead people walking at first until he saw that big zombie in the road.

The zombie must have been nearly seven foot tall and as big as a house with it. The shirt it wore was ripped open to reveal its ribs and innards some of its intestines nearly spilling onto the road. Its pasty face turned at the sound of Barry's van, and

Barry saw the white eyes and the blood oozing from its dead lips. Barry had run right into the thing and lost control, and crashed into a tree. Luckily, he was unhurt and was out of the van quickly, and as he looked at the road, he saw the big zombie trying to get to its feet, but its back was broken. The thing was still reaching out for Barry the damned thing still wanted to feed on him.

Barry had run and then he came upon a house where he took some cans of food and an axe which he found in the garden shed.

Chloe was with her boyfriend Tim at the time of the outbreak they had been watching the television when the reporter told them of the zombies. Tim had said he was going out to get his mother and father, and he would be back for her. She lived alone in a one-bedroom flat, and she waited for him, but he never came back. She had packed a rucksack with food, and a hammer from her draw in the kitchen a useful item.

Then she had hit the streets and tired to stay away from the zombies. She headed into the countryside, and came upon her first zombie. She was walking around a large tree and she almost went straight into it! The zombie was a small girl and it hissed at Chloe like an animal. Chloe had surprised even herself as she calmly took out the hammer, and put it with force into the top of the girl's head. That's what the reporter had said kill the brain, and you kill the zombie.

The poor little zombie girl looked somehow sad laying dead in her summer dress which was splattered with blood her blonde dirty hair spread out around her. Then Chloe had walked and walked until her feet ached, and then she had run into Barry. The man had held up his hands and said to her.

"Hey lady I'm a human, zombies don't talk remember."

She had smiled at the tall thin man, and that was that they travelled together.

==

That night they found an old maintenance shed by the side of the motorway. The day had been a good one in the fact that they had not seen too many zombies on the motorway, a lot of crashed cars which they stayed away from.

Barry put an iron bar against the door and jammed it shut that would keep out any zombie that tried the door. The maintenance shed was small, and there was nothing inside the shed was bare. Barry sat on the floor and Chloe followed suit.

"You know what I miss Barry."

"No tell me."

"Music, I loved my music the eighties were a favourite, and the Irish band *U2*."

She smiled at the thought of listening to music once more and dancing in the night clubs.

"I miss the movies I love watching movies especially horror movies."

"You have to talk about horror at a time like this Barry really."

He laughed and then remembered her hatred of clowns and smiled as he said, "So you must have watched movies with clowns in them."

Chloe shivered at the thought clowns scared the hell out of her. She remembered once at a Halloween party a mate of hers had come as a clown, she had left the party at once. Barry went on.

"Yes, zombie world that series it and of course the classic *poltergeist*."

"Oh, Barry please no more talk of horror movies and zombies we have real zombies now for god's sake."

Barry could hear the anger and fear in her voice and decided it would be a good idea to shut the hell up.

"I'm sorry Chloe I took that to far."

"Yes, you did now let's get some sleep."

==

They left the maintenance shed in the morning and made their way along the motorway. They hid as they saw a zombie walking between the crashed cars it was an old woman with white hair, and wearing only her panties. Her sagging breasts almost reached her belly button, and as she walked past, they saw the ripped and torn skin of her back they could see the spinal column.

"Come on let's move it," Barry said getting away from the old woman. They passed a bridge on their right, and as they walked on two zombies came out at them from behind an over turned van.

"Watch out Chloe," Barry cried out as a zombie reached out for her. The zombie was a once handsome man wearing a black suit his hair was still neatly combed back. His white eyes seemed to look at her as he reached out. Chloe moved backwards, and took out the hammer and swung it in an arc. The hammer end smacked the handsome zombie in the side of the jaw, and it went down on the ground its jaw now dislocated and hanging. Chloe stepped forwards and using the claw end of the hammer put it deep into the zombie's brain.

Barry watched all this as he dealt with the second zombie a woman with huge breasts, and wearing as low-cut top and mini skirt. Half of her face had been eaten away, but he could tell that once she had been a pretty little thing. The big breasted zombie hissed at him, and came towards him Barry backed off and let the zombie come at him. He gripped his axe and when she was close, he lifted it over his head, and it slammed down hard into the top of her head.

"Come on Chloe let's keep moving," he said looking at the two dead zombies.

"God will this ever end," Chloe sobbed, but followed Barry away from the scene.

Out of the corner of her eye she saw the old white haired naked zombie woman coming back their way, and moved off in a hurry catching up with Barry.

==

As they neared a city they stopped, and Barry scratched his head and looked at Chloe, "I say we head into the city it will be so much quicker."

Chloe didn't like the thought of going into a city far too many zombies, and nowhere to hide.

"I think we would be foolish to enter a city lets go round it."

Barry shook his head he had made up his mind, "No I say the city and passing through we can pick up supplies."

He had a point they had not much food left and water was down to the last bottle. Chloe sighed and said, "Okay then but let's do it quickly I don't want to spend too much time in a city of the dead."

==

They reached the city and walked quickly down the street they saw shop fronts smashed open, and cars crashed all over the roads.

"This is horrible Barry," Chloe wined as they saw zombies walking along the pathways on both sides of the street.

"Damn it there are too many zombies," he cursed.

"I told you that lets turn back then."

They turned back and gasped there was a gang of zombies blocking the way back, and coming towards them moaning and hissing the sound was awful. The dead had arms missing and one had no jaw just its upper teeth another had a missing leg, and crawled along the ground after them.

"Come on," Barry said and grabbed Chloe's hand and ran onwards deeper into the city. Barry saw the shop out of the corner of his eye as more zombies blocked the way up ahead, they were trapped. There was an office block on the left-hand side, but the front door was well blocked up with boxes shopping trolleys you name it.

On the right-hand side there was a fancy dress shop and the shop front was intact. Barry headed for the fancy dress shop, and pulled Chloe inside and shut the door and locked it. Zombies began to bang on the glass door, and the glass of the shops show case.

"They will break the glass Barry," Chloe cried out as the sound intensified.

More and more zombies were at the shop front and the glass began to show silvers as it began to slowly break under the pounding of the zombies.

"We need to go up to the flat above," Barry said and saw a door way that must lead upstairs. Chloe followed Barry and shivered as she passed a clown's suit hanging up waiting for some fancy-dress goer to purchase. Barry opened the door, and screamed as three clown zombies poured out! Chloe was right behind him, and both were taken by surprise as the

zombies came upon them. Chloe just froze as all her worst
nightmares happened in that one second as the clowns came
out at them. Barry was bitten on the check, and cried out as
his flesh was ripped away from the bone. Chloe fell to the
floor a big clown zombie on top of her clawing at her long
hair.

The other zombie took a chuck out of her leg, and she
screamed. Then the glass caved in at the front of the shop, and
the zombies from the street poured into the fancy dress shop
to join in on the feast.

Chapter fourteen

Newspaper

Max saw the two people go into the fancy dress shop from his window high up in the small office building. It was the same building that Chloe and Barry had seen with all the shopping trolleys, and various other junk piled up at the door way. Max sighed the two people were dead that was for sure, he saw the number of zombies that rushed the shop banging on the door and windows they would soon break in. He had been watching the fancy dress shop, the owner and his two sons had shut themselves upstairs, and dressed in clown costumes why they did this he didn't know.

Then the old man must have died because he only saw two for a while then he saw three. Only now they were all dead it was obvious from the way they moved around the flat above the shop. He watched the shop, and then saw the three clown zombies disappear from sight, the two people must have opened the doorway to the flat above. Then the zombies broke the window at the front of the store, and they piled inside moaning and making terrible noises.

Max could watch no more he was sick of living in this world why him why now. He had just made himself a success when the outbreak happened, he had been promoted in the newspaper to editor, and he was getting married to a beautiful Indian woman he had met on line.

Things had been looking good For Max now he was a dead man thanks to the fucking zombies.

There had been five of them at the start, and they had come up with the idea of writing a note telling people to join them, and photo coping hundreds of sheets. The building had a helicopter pad at the top, and the pilot was holed up with them.

The helicopter had left the building with the sheets three days ago and not returned, but Max and the other two had seen the flames in the distance.

==

Jerry put the helicopter down by the petrol station the bird was running out of gas and needed fuel. Gibbs got out of the cockpit, and along with Jerry they walked over to inspect the pumps. Jerry was a small slight man who looked like a strong gust of wind might blow him over. Gibbs on the other hand was a large well-built man with a boyish face that made him look younger than he was.

"Hey Jerry man I think I found one that is good."

Jerry came over and both men didn't see the zombies coming out of one of the storage sheds close by.

"Yes, this will do mate let's get moving," Jerry replied.

Gibbs turned and saw the zombies!

"Fucking hell mate," he shouted and the zombies homed in on him.

Jerry made a run for the helicopter and managed to get inside and close both doors. Gibbs tried to run, but tripped, and fell to the ground the zombies fell on top of him. He screamed as zombies took chunks of flesh out of his arms and throat one zombie ripped open his stomach, and put its hand inside reaching for the intestines. Gibbs blood splattered the zombies as they fed on his fresh flesh.

Jerry got the helicopter in the air, and then screamed as a girl zombie tore into his throat from behind. She must have sneaked in while they were at the pumps, blood spurted over the window scene and the helicopter went down. It crashed into the still screaming body of Gibbs and the horde of zombies that surrounded him, and exploded in a ball of flames that went high into the sky.

==

Max was lost in thought then there was Dave and Carol they had gone out to get more supplies two days ago, and not come back. Dave was careful as they opened the back door to the building there were a lot of zombies walking aimlessly about. He went quickly outside and hid behind a car Carol followed him. They had worked together on the newspaper for many years, and had become friends. Dave often invited Carol and her boyfriend Andy over for dinner, and likewise for Carol inviting him and Andrea his wife.

But both had not seen or heard from their loved ones since the outbreak, and it seemed like a good idea to hole themselves up in the office.

Dave moved off quickly and Carol followed, but the zombies had seen them and moaned out loud as if it was a signal to other zombies that there was a running meal. Dave panicked he hadn't had any contact with the zombies nor had Carol, and they realized then that this had been a massive mistake there were far too many zombies. Dave found a car that was open and jumped inside and locked the door, poor Carol banged on the glass and screamed at him to let her in.

Dave had soiled his underpants and was crying like a little baby as he watched the zombies tear Carol apart. They tore off her arms and legs and dragged them away to a quiet spot to feed on them. Her insides were taken out by another group of zombies, and they sat on the ground eating them.

Dave was sick was well and the inside of the car stank of shit and sick. One zombie picked up a large stone and Dave cried as it put the stone through the side window. Zombies crawled inside the car, and Dave screamed as they grabbed him.

==

Max finished the last tin of cold chicken and leek soup now he had nothing left to eat, and the water was down to the last bottle. He knew that he needed to go out for supplies, but he couldn't face the zombies he just wasn't strong enough for that. He sat there looking out of the office window a few of the zombies had even managed to move some of the blockade at the office front door maybe they were learning too.

Two days later and Max was now at his wits end he could not stay like this, die inside an office building, but he couldn't go outside either. He knew it was the end for him the game was up as they say. He felt sad because his life had been on the up when this shit had happened, and he cursed the zombies.

"Fucking zombies I hate them."

He sighed this was how it was going to end then. He stood up and looked around the silent office once more, and a sob escaped him. He remembered the office party in this very room only a while ago, and how he had got off with Judy the temp with the massive tits. Man, she was a handful and when she had rubbed his cock through his trousers, he thought it was going to be his night, but someone had caught them. So, he had gone back to the party red faced and got drunk, and Judy had gone home with some bloody young student who had a part time job.

He crawled onto the window ledge and looked down it seemed so far to the hard concrete below. He closed his eyes and let his body fall.

The world did not flash before his eyes he would have liked it too.

He would have loved to see this life replayed and to experience the good times only of course. But it never happened he felt the cold and the wind slamming against his body, and then the hard jolt as he hit the ground at speed. His head hurt like hell, and his body ached in some places, and was numb in others.

He was conscious, and could hear the moaning zombies coming ever closer moaning as they came.

Chapter fifteen

Glenn

Glenn lived above the butchers just down from the fancy dress shop, and facing the office block. He watched from his parents building as the man jumped from the window, and fell to the ground with a thud, and then as he hit the ground blood sprayed out around him. It looked like a kind of giant pizza on the hard ground, and then the zombies moved in. Then he saw the man's arm move damn he was still alive as the zombies began to tear pieces of flesh from his body and eat them.

Glenn looked away why had he jumped the fool if he had known he was in the office he would have tried to join the man, but now it was too late. Glenn lived above the butcher shop, and it had been once with his parents, it was only a stop gap until they could afford something better, they had told him. Then before the outbreak his parents had found a house, but they needed to be patient as they had to wait until the owner found a house there was a chain involved.

So, they had stayed in the flat above the butchers then the outbreak had happened, and his parents had never returned from work. He was sixteen with short dark hair and an oriental look about him that would be from his mother's side.

Her family came from China.

He was a small young man, but that had never bothered him as he was fit and agile. When the outbreak had first happened, he had robbed the butchers shop below before the looters had moved in and took what they liked. He had cooked all the meat and frozen it, but then the power supply had gone off.

He had eaten most of the defrosted meat, but had to throw away a lot as well.

He now managed on canned food, and often went out to get supplies he was fast on his feet, and could dodge the slow zombies, but he still feared them. He had not killed one yet, but had heard on the news before the power went out that you had to kill the brain. He had found a camping cooker and gas cinder, and now cooked his meals on that most of the time it was hot tinned soup. He was running out of bottled water now, but he wanted to move from the flat, and get out of the city which was overrun by the dead.

==

To pass the time Glenn played games with the zombies, first when the outbreak had happened, he had barricaded the door which led up to the flat. Putting tables and chairs, and anything he could move down the stairs on his side of the door. Once he was secure, he had to think up some games to keep him occupied.

One game involved a bowling ball tied tightly with rope.

When the zombies came close, he would throw the bowling ball out of the window, and hit them on the head. Maybe because it was surrounded by rope and cushioned the blow but the zombies always got back to their feet. Then he would pull in the bowling ball, and watch for the next zombie that moved close.

Then he would use his sling shot and fire painted nuts at the zombies. Always aiming for the head, and pretending that they dropped dead when it hit them in the head. That night he went to sleep dreaming of the zombie Olympics.

He was lined up with a row of tied up zombies then a gun went, and the zombies were released. He raced down the track and won the race easily the zombies milling around looking for hot flesh. He was in the boxing ring wearing a head guard and in the other corner a zombie the bell went. He hit the zombie again and again until it hit the floor, and took an eight count then the bell went. Handlers got rope round the zombie and pulled it back to the corner.

Then he got ready for the next round he would win this easy, but then the banging started.

He woke up and looked out of the window. Zombies were moving in mass inside the butcher shop, and banging on his door maybe he had been snoring loudly or moaning in his sleep.

Anyway, it was time to go.

==

He packed his rucksack with tinned cans of soup and meat and fish plus a kitchen knife and clever. He took a change of trousers and t-shirt and under pants also he took his mother's medical kit. He looked out of the window, and saw the drain pipe leading up to the roof of the building. He gripped the drain pipe and moved upwards it was only a few feet to the roof, and he gripped the side at the top and pulled himself over. The roof was flat, and a shed like door way stood in the centre which was closed. The shops were all attached and he went from one shop roof to the next until he reached the last one. Then he climbed down the last drain pipe and saw the motor way stretching off into the distance, and the wooded countryside close by.

He headed into the woods.

==

"Wow this is so cool," he said as he raced through the woods breathing in the fresh air.

He saw a huge oak tree and began to climb the trunk; he reached the first large branch, and decided this is where he would sleep. He kept waking up during the night the sounds from the woods were alien to him, and some frightening. He thought he heard zombies close by at one point and looked down, but it was far too dark.

Next morning, he climbed down and walked through the trees until he came to a small town. It had a main high street and roads going off it. He couldn't see any sign post so didn't know what small town it was, but maybe he could get some more supplies. Then a large man grabbed him from behind and put a knife to his throat.

"You move kid and I will cut your throat open."

But then the man relaxed his grip on the boy.

"Please mister I am just looking for food."

"Just go kid and keep running if I see you again, I will kill you."

Glenn didn't like the sound of the man's voice, and ran as fast as he could.

Chapter sixteen
Mad dog Anthony

Anthony mad dog Maloney was a big man in every department. He was well over six foot six, and as wide as a house he had a bald shiny head, and a thick bushy beard. It had once been just a goatee, but in these times, he couldn't be bothered to shave and let it grow wild. He had dark mean looking eyes set in a hard looking face with acne scars on his cheeks a reminder from his youth. He stood and watched as the kid ran away from him, he was not about to become a child killer no way or a woman killer for that matter. He did have some principles which he kept too.

If it had been a man, it would have been different, and he probably would have cut the guy's throat without flinching. He wore a dirt black suit without a tie and carried a night stick in his belt, and a sword strapped to his back in a sheaf.

He had been an ex-boxer and a wrestler back in the day before things turned bad. His boxing career was short lived he started well with five wins all by knock out, but then in his sixth fight he got thrown out for hitting his opponent while he was on the canvas. After that he turned to wrestling, and did well always playing the mean bad guy which, the crowds loved. Then when the breakout occurred, he was into being a body guard for the rich and famous.

He remembered the first time he encountered the zombies he had been helping a young film star. The guy was good looking, but such a spoilt brat and they had been running like hell down an alley way having been caught off guard by the horde of zombies while trying to get into the limo. It had been a dead end, and the two of them looked at the oncoming zombies.

Young and old among them an old woman still holding a rolling pin and wearing an apron. A fat man with half his jaw missing a young girl with her arm missing up to the elbow. He then made a decision which would save his life he turned to the young actor and said, "Sorry."

The young man looked confused and then Anthony hit him hard on the jaw the actor went down in a heap. The big man picked him up and lifted the actor over his head, and threw him at the oncoming zombies. The actor screamed as the zombies started to feast on his warm flesh. It gave Anthony the room he needed, and he ran past the zombies that were now only interested in the warm bundle at their feet. That had been a close call, and later he had found the sword above someone's fire place in a house he holed up in for a while.

The night stick he found on the dead body of a policeman.

==

He walked down the main street of the small town hoping not to see the kid again. He came to a school and stopped might be a good place to look for supplies. He stopped outside and looked at the words writing on the wall, 'A teacher's purpose is not to create students in his or her image, but to develop students who can create their own image.'

"Very true," he said out loud.

He entered the school the front doors were wide open not a good sign. He walked down the corridor and stopped as he saw two zombies round a corner up ahead, and come towards him. One of the zombies wore a ripped dress blood all over her exposed stomach, and the other had a janitors suit on which was covered in blood and gore.

Anthony drew his sword and raced to meet the zombies he screamed as he cut the janitors head off. Then he cut the woman in half, and pushed the end of the sword into her forehead. He walked up to the janitors head the head was looking around, and moving its lips, and cut it in half. He was so engrossed in his work that he didn't hear the small girl behind him. The zombie girl bit into his leg her teeth going through his suit trousers, and into his calf muscle.

"Oh, shit no way," he cursed out loud.

He looked down at the zombie girl she wore a plain white t-shirt and white shorts as if she were doing P.E when she got attacked. He sighed as she came towards him, and then he cut her in half with one strong blow.

==

More zombies came out of the corridor some from round the bend up ahead others from open door ways. He limped back and saw more zombies blocking the exit door. He saw the principal's office it looked all clear and limped inside, and locked the door behind him. What a damned fool he had been never go into buildings especially not in towns or cities.

The office was empty save from a desk and two chairs, and a filing cabinet over against one wall. He looked at his calf the bite was deep and blood pooled around the wound. That was it his life was over he just had to wait now for the change.

He started to feel hot.

He was on a boat a large and expensive boat, and he was with his girlfriend who it turned out was a famous model. Life was brilliant, and he enjoyed sailing the seas with his girl away from the land of the dead. He sipped a double martini and looked across at his girl she was topless, and her small pointy breasts stood up like coat hangers. She wore small bikini bottoms that didn't hide much, and he was getting hard looking at her slim body.

"Come here love."

"What do you want big boy."

She came over to him and went into his arms he held her tight and kissed her on the mouth. He forced his tongue inside her throat, and then stopped and drew back. Blood gushed out of his mouth and he stared in horror as the green skinned zombie in front of him chewed on his tongue!

He woke up in a cold sweat.

"What the fuck."

==

He woke up later and felt cold he pressed his arm with his hand it was cold. He felt his pulse there was no pulse.

"Holy shit I'm a zombie," he said laughing. But he could still think and feel as well, when he touched his arms and legs, he could feel them. He got to his feet and walked to the door his legs were stiff, and it was hard to walk properly. He opened the door, and the zombies looked at him, and then started to shamble away. Some pushed past him and went into the office, but most just went away in all directions losing interest in him now.

He saw a mirror in one room and walked up to it his eyes were pure white and his skin pale and ghost like. He sobbed as he looked at his image, he was indeed a zombie, but a thinking feeling zombie. He walked out of the school, and into the play ground area. Then he saw a woman close by she held a machete in her hand.

"Hey no I'm not a real zombie," he tried to say but it came out like a moan. Then he felt intense pain as his head was cut off and it rolled across the play ground and came to a stop. He saw the woman standing over him with the machete posed and then darkness.

Chapter seventeen

Show no mercy

She chopped the big zombies head into two with her machete and smiled the big fucker was chopped down to size now. Blue was her name, and nothing else she forgot her real name ages ago and never used anything but blue. She enjoyed killing zombies in fact she thought it was fun, and didn't miss the old world at all. The only way to live was on the edge, and in this new world that's exactly what happened every day.

She tried not to think of her past life she had been used by many men, and was a man hater. She had started dating at sixteen and found that boys didn't stay with her long okay she was a bit crazy even back then. She had gone through many men by the time she left college, and went into to real world as her dad would say. She got a job stacking shelves in the local supermarket, and had a long line of boyfriends here. She got a reputation for sleeping around, and was often called an old slag or the supermarket bike.

Then she fell in love with a handsome man who wanted to be an actor it had lasted for three years. She had fallen for him badly and he promised to marry her, but as he got more roles in the movies so he got more women. He had dumped her, and she had been shattered, but she picked herself up, and then the outbreak had happened. She soon found that she was a ruthless killer and soon enjoyed the killing.

She was in her thirties with short blonde hair and blue eyes and a real looker with her pale white skin, and large eye lashes, and full red lips. She walked out of the school play ground and out of the small town. This was her world now and she showed no mercy.

==

Blue walked down the country lane, and heard no birds singing she had never thought about it before. But she hadn't heard the birds singing for age's maybe they were zombies as well she had seen zombie dogs on her travels. She spotted three zombies in a field close by, and climbed over the wooden fence. She took out her machete, and called out to the zombies, "Hey dead heads over here."

The zombies turned at her voice, and slowly came towards her. One of them a male was rotten, his face was almost skeletal, and you could see his rib cage through his ruined chest. Another was a woman with a large chunk taken out of her throat, blood covered her white coat. The last zombie was another man, but he looked fresh he wore a business suit, and had black curly hair she couldn't see any bite marks on him.

Maybe he had a heart attack or died from natural causes whatever you would still turn. She approached the skeletal zombie first, and cut its head off she kicked the woman zombie to the ground. The fresh zombie came at her.

"Come on handsome want some," she teased it.

As it came close, she put the machete into its head, and the zombie in the suit went down. She kicked the woman zombie in the head it was trying to get to its feet. Then she sliced the top of the woman's head off and it lay still then she went over to the skeletal zombie, and put the end of the machete through its brain.

==

She found a farm house just as night was falling, and after a quick check round to see if it was all clear she locked the doors and windows. She slept in the double bed, and had the best sleep she had for a long while. But throughout the night she would wake to the sound of banging, but she thought nothing of it only zombies trying to get in.

Next morning, she ate some tuna from a tin, and heard the banging once more it was coming from a cupboard in the hall. She sighed and took out the machete, and went to the cupboard and opened it and stepped back. Two zombie kids came out at her and caught her off guard they grabbed at her legs, and tried to bite her through the thick jeans.

"Little fuckers," she cursed at them.

She pushed at the boy zombie, and it went tumbling to the floor. She took hold of the girl zombie and picked it up by the brown long hair it kept trying to reach out to her. Blue looked at the greenish rotten face of the once cute girl, and put the machete into its eye and through its brain. The boy zombie had gotten to its feet, and with one swift movement she took off its head. She put the blade of the machete into its severed head.

"Bloody zombies," she cried out.

==

Blue walked through the country side it was a windy cold day and it looked like rain soon, the sky was very dark over head. She would have to find some kind of shelter soon she didn't like getting wet. She saw a zombie close by and crouched down in some bushes and watched it amble by. It was one ugly zombie both cheeks had been eaten through, and you could see its teeth standing out. Its side was ripped open and it had no insides probably eaten in a zombie feast.

But the zombie moved, and even looked right at her as it passed, but she was quiet and it walked on. She stood up and was about to carry on when she heard some screaming close by. It sounded like children, and zombies didn't scream.

She ran into the trees and heard the screaming again it was just up ahead. She came out of the trees and into a field and saw two small children surrounded by four zombies. She breathed deeply, and took out the machete and walked over to the first zombie she put the machete into the top of its head. Next, she sliced the throat of a petrol attendant zombie, and as it tried to grab her, she cut its hand off. But still it came she composed herself, and put the machete into its forehead.

The other two zombies were coming for her now!

She went down and swivelled her leg on the ground and took out the closest zombie's legs it fell down heavily. She stood and sliced off the top of the zombie's head it stood for a second with its hands trying to find the top of its head, then it collapsed. The last zombie was still on the ground and she jumped on top of it, and the zombie tried to bite her, its breath was foul. She pushed the zombies head down and took a moment its breath had made her feel sick, and she gagged.

Then she breathed fresh air, and put the machete into its head.

She got up and looked over at the two kids.

==

She didn't need any hangers on even if they were kids, she would make sure they were okay, and then put them on their way.

"I'm blue," she said to them.

"I'm Jake and his is my sister Lucy," said the young boy.

Jake was seventeen he was a thin boy of medium height with spiky hair and green eyes. His sister Lucy was a small eight-year-old black hair and green eyes, and a very cute face she was like a delicate porcelain figure.

"Our parents died and," the boy began.

"I don't want to hear your life story I have no time for that," she said sternly to him.

She unpacked some tinned tuna and spam, and gave it to the boy they both had rucksacks.

"Now you go and take care okay."

"But you can't just leave us," the boy said looking around the field.

"Please miss we are hopeless on our own," the little girl pleaded.

Blue shook her head no. She saw an ugly zombie coming out of the trees the screams must have attracted it. She walked towards it, and put the machete into its eye ball it went down.

"You two take care."

Then blue run into the trees and was gone. She couldn't have anyone else with her it was the survival of the fittest, and looking after number one only.

Chapter eighteen

Jake and Lucy

Jake and Lucy watched as the woman disappeared into the trees. He couldn't believe that the woman what was her name 'blue' had just left them. He took his sister small hand in his he had to be the adult now, and he gently pulled her along after the woman into the trees. But it was no good the woman was gone, and they walked through the trees that afternoon trying to find her.

That early evening, they sat down in the hollow of a large tree and rested.

"How will we survive?" Lucy asked him

Jake shook his head from side to side he really didn't know, but he had to show Lucy he was strong.

"Don't you worry you have big brother to look after you."

"I know but I want mummy and daddy."

He sighed he knew that was coming, "They have gone to a far better place now Lucy."

The outbreak had happened while they were on the way back from visiting their grannies. Their dad a big man was driving when someone ran into the road he swerved and hit a tree. The two kids were wearing seat belts in the back, but their mother wasn't, and she went through the window shield and hit the tree hard breaking her neck. She was dead and so was father he lay slumped over the steering wheel blood pouring out of a wound on his head.

They were close to home, and Jake had managed to get them back.

After a few days the zombies were worse, and then he saw their mother in the garden, but it wasn't her. She stumbled on with her neck at a funny angle. He didn't want Lucy to see so he had packed up their rucksacks, and they had hit the road. They had been on the road for a week now dodging the slow zombies, and then the woman had been the first human they had seen.

Now she was gone and they were on their own again. Jake put his arm round his sister's shoulders, and the two kids slept in the hollow of the tree.

==

They ate tuna and cold *chicken soup,* and then walked on through the trees they came to a field and stopped. There were about a dozen zombies in the field just aimlessly walking about and moaning.

"We better go back in the woods and try and go round the side of them," the woods stretched far away into the distance by the side of the field.

He knew they were running out of tinned food and bottled water, and would have to find supplies soon. They found a stream in the afternoon and both bathed their hands, and face's the cool water felt so good on their skin. Jake opened a tin of tuna with the can opener, and they ate it half each. As they were finishing, they heard a splash, and from the other side of the stream came two zombies.

They entered the shallow stream, and came towards the two kids moaning as they came. One zombie had an arm missing and the side of its head was blown away. The other was naked and it had a gaping hole where its penis should have been. Jake put on his rucksack and took his sisters hand, and they ran back into the trees.

They came to a main road and waited in the bushes, and looked at the road. They saw no zombies on the road, and Jake decided it would be a good idea to follow the road it might lead to a town where they could get supplies.

Then he heard a noise and grabbed Lucy, and ran back into the bushes and watched. A truck speed past with four punk like men in the back screaming at the top of their lungs, and making funny noises. They looked scary with their spiked hair and painted faces, and Lucy held onto him tight.

==

Jake took Lucy's hand and they ran down the road, and almost ran into an oncoming car. The car screeched to a stop in front of them and Jake just stared at the driver it was a woman. The woman got out of the car and cried, "Oh my god little ones."

She came to them and hugged them both, "What are you doing alone?"

The woman had red hair and a pale face she was a pleasant looking woman a bit on the plump side, but Jake liked her instantly.

"Our parents are in heaven," Lucy said hugging the lady back.

"Oh, you poor mites."

"Can we come with you lady," Jake asked.

"Of course, you must get in the car."

She looked at the woods on each side of the road, and hurried to the car.

==

The small cottage had a steel fence around it and the zombies banged on the fence as Jake and Lucy got out of the car in the drive.

"Damn things get more and more of them each day."

Stacy that was her name had driven near to the gate, and pressed her horn the zombies had moved to the car. Then she had pressed a button and the gates opened she had driven through, and shut them, but it had been close. She made them hot soup she had a gas cooker from her camping days and the soup was good.

"You will be safe here Jake," she said to him.

He nodded his head enjoying the hot food.

"I like you Stacy," Lucy said with a smile.

"Good because I like the both of you too."

Stacy had bought the cottage five years ago, and had been on holiday from her job in the city when the outbreak happened. At first it had been easy to get supplies, but lately more and more zombies had hit the countryside. It was as if they were tired of the cities or they had empted the cities of humans, and now seeked them out in the countryside. Stacy didn't tell the kids, but she had a bad feeling about a group of men close by. They kept driving by the cottage, and howling at her.

They looked like bad people with their spiked hair dos and painted up faces.

==

They sat at the table the next morning and Stacy done them eggs on toast which the kids gulped down hungrily. The night had been the best so far for the kids they had shared a bed in the guest room, and slept soundly for the first time in weeks.

"Now kids what shall we do today."

"I want to check on the hen's eggs," Lucy beamed.

Then all hell broke loose as a loud explosion hit the cottage and all three of them were thrown to the floor. Dust and rubble were all around them, and Jake couldn't see at first then he heard the moaning. Then the shooting began and soon the dust cleared and Jake saw Stacy holding Lucy close fear in her eyes.

Then the men with spiked hair came into view, and took Stacy and Lucy away.

"Hey leave them alone." Jake cursed at them. One of the punks came up to him, and sniffed him like a dog.

"Get this one in the back of the truck too," he ordered. His face was painted red with white rings around his eyes, and he looked one mean mother.

Chapter nineteen

Survival of the fittest

The camp was in a huge field the surrounding area was fenced off with high metal fencing. The three prisoners were brought into the camp blind folded, and only when they were inside the blind folds were taken off, and they could see the huge field. It was like a camp site a gipsy camp site, and they could see two big fires with pots of stew burning over them the smell was lovely cooking meat and vegetables.

Painted men and women were all over the camp it seemed if you wanted to be part of the gang you had to be painted up. Cries and screams erupted from the painted people every so often, that seemed to be normal to them. Jake and Lucy were given to an old woman who took them away to a tent by the edge of the field. Jake held his sister's little hand, and smiled at her looking at her cute face and said, "Don't worry Lucy we will be fine here."

"But the painted men scare me, Jake."

"No don't be scared if they were going to hurt us, they would have by now."

"Okay Jake."

Stacy was taken to another tent a bigger tent and she was led there by two goons with spiked hair. She entered the tent and saw the huge man sitting on a wooden throne he held a stick in his hand, and looked at the woman before him. He was a dark-skinned man with a bald, and his face was covered in paint in all kinds of weird shapes and lines he looked evil.

His massive belly hung over his trousers, and threatened to bulge out of his dirty white shirt.

"I am the 'cat' I am the leader here."

"I am Stacy sir."

He looked over her body and smiled she felt like she was naked before his roaming eyes.

"The rules are simple you pass a test and you can stay."

He paused looking her up and down again and licking his lips.

"If you stay you must be painted and stay that way."

He sighed, "If you pass and stay you will be given a job and you will be expected to carry out that job and in return you will be fed and housed, and of course protected from the dead."

He signalled the guards to take her away. She was put into a cage with others, and then she saw Jake and Lucy, and ran over to them and hugged them both.

"Where did you go," she asked them.

"Some crazy woman took us to a tent and gave us some food," Jake replied.

Lucy added, "And then they put us in here."

Lucy sobbed and looked around the cage there were about ten others in the cage, and it had no roof if it rained, they were being kept like animals.

"I don't like it in here," Lucy sobbed.

"It's okay darling I will find a way out," Stacy smiled at the little girl and brushed her hair away from her face.

"And I don't like that," Jake said pointing.

Stacy followed his finger and saw other cages close by, but these ones were full of zombies.

==

An hour later a man was dragged out of the cage by two goons who screamed at the others as they took them. The man was small and weedy looking with receding hair, and large round eyes that looked about him in terror. Stacy and the kids watched as the man was taken over to a pit, they could see zombies being lowered into the pit.

"No please I beg you," the man pleaded.

"Shut up scum," a painted goon spat at the man and dragged him over to the edge of the pit. The cat man sat on a wooden throne near the pit, and held his stick he had a robe round his shoulders, and tried to look like a king.

"Throw him in if he survives, he can stay," the king shouted out. People with painted faces had gathered round the pit also, and they were screaming and crying out with blood lust. The man was thrown into the pit, and the people and the king watched. He screamed out in agony, and Stacy guessed the zombies had gotten him.

"Useless no spine at all," the king hissed from his throne.

"What good would he have been to us," he added.

The people cheered the king and bowed to him, and he sat there with his massive belly, and smiled at them all lapping up the applause. Another man was dragged out of the cage he was bigger than the last man, but he looked old and had grey hair, and a wrinkled-up face.

"Please have mercy I am old and can't fight, but I can do other things."

"Shut up scum bag talk when you are spoken too," and a spiked haired gone kicked the old man in the stomach and then dragged him over to a metal pipe. The pipe had been cut in half the man was pushed into the pipe holding his belly and moaning out loud. When the man reached the middle zombies were put in from both sides.

"Now get out of the pipe and you live," the king shouted his belly moving like a huge jelly. The people began to scream and shout. The grey-haired man was no match for the zombies, and he was soon taken apart, blood spraying over some of the painted spec takers.

"Another useless piece of shit," the king shouted out.

"Have we no good new comers to join us," he added and tapped his stick on the ground. The cage was opened again and this time Stacy was grabbed Jake stepped forwards and grabbed the spiky haired man's arm and shouted, "Leave her alone."

"Fuck off kid," and the spiky haired man hit Jake. Jake cried out and held his face as the cage was closed, and he watched as the man dragged Stacy away.

==

Stacy was put into a fenced of area it was round and about ten feet across from one fence to the next. She was given a wooden pole like a snooker cue, and the painted people surrounded the fenced off area screaming and shouting. The king watched from his throne on a wooden platform. Three zombies were pushed into the fenced off area. A thin zombie with just wisps of hair on its head, and one eye missing came to her Stacy hit the zombie with the cue, and then kicked it over.

Another zombie with its insides missing grabbed at her she hit it with the stick it too went down, but the other one was getting up again. The third zombie was a woman wearing a mini skirt and small top she had been pretty once, but now her face was turning green, and her skin was peeling off in strips.

Stacy hit the woman and it went down this time Stacy plunged down with the stick, and it buried itself in the zombie's head. The people screamed around her and Stacy was getting out of breath now the other two zombies were coming for her.

"Enough," the king shouted out.

The zombies were immediately taken out by two goons with poles with a hoop of rope at the end.

"Bring her to my tent she is mine."

With that the king stood, and made his way to the tent five goons following him.

==

The next morning Jake was awakened by the cage door opening, and the spiked haired man coming in and grabbing him.

"Hey," Jake shouted as the others started to wake up. Lucy was taken as well, but the kids were frog marched not dragged. Jake sobbed as he held his sister's hand what horror awaited them, what fate. They were led over to a large tent and were pushed in from behind. They saw the huge dark man sitting on a wooden throne, and Stacy standing next to him smiling down at them.

"It's okay kids you are safe now," Stacy said to them.

"I don't understand," Jake replied looking at the fat king.

"It's okay we can all stay and be one happy family," she beamed at the two kids. Later that day the king left the tent and the three of them were alone.

"That mean bastard," Stacy sobbed.

"What s up Stacy, I thought you liked him," Lucy asked her.

"It's an act dear the man is a mindless brute."

"Great I didn't like him either," Jake smiled.

Stacy didn't tell the kids, but the man had raped her last night it had been awful, and she had bruises under her clothes. His big smelly body on top of hers and his big penis pushing up inside her, but she had let him have his way with her.

She had asked him to spare the kids, and she would do anything for him, and he believed her he was a simple oaf. Stacy had been looking out at the metal fences, and she saw hundreds of zombies clawing at them. The camp had been lazy for a few days, and not gone out and butchered the dead now they were here in force.

==

It was easy to get out of the tent even with two goons guarding the front entrance. What they didn't realize was you only had to life the tent from the base and craw under and out. Stacy took Jake and Lucy's hands, and they sneaked away from the large tent these savages were mindless animals and that was all. She had seen a supply shed earlier, and she quickly headed for this now.

The shed was open and they all went inside and she closed the door. The fence was only a foot away from the shed and the zombies moaned loudly, and clawed at the fence looking for their next meal.

"Right kids we are getting out of here."

"Great stuff," Jake beamed.

"I am going to cut the fence now you have to be really quick you both understand."

"I'm scared," Lucy sobbed.

"No, you have to be strong or these men will kill us," Stacy said holding the small girl's hand.

"And besides we will get out where there are not too many zombies around okay."

"Yes, sis just follow us and we will be fine," Jake said smiling at her.

Stacy picked up a pair of wire cutters and smiled, "Show time."

They could see out of the shed it had one dirty window, and they waited until the king got back. He was driven into the compound in a white van with no roof he sat in the back on another wooden throne his belly wobbling like crazy. The painted people screamed and shouted as the king arrived, and the zombies were getting more animated and angrier.

Stacy came out of the shed with the two kids and went over to a patch of fence with no zombies she cut the metal wire. She pushed the kids through the hole, and then got out herself zombies were coming for them now. She quickly made the hole bigger and shouted, "Come and get it."

She took the kids hands and ran off into the woods a few of the zombies followed them the rest went into the hole in the fence.

==

The spiky haired man stood guard at the tent entrance, and saw the king arrive. He was second in command and loved his king, and he would do anything for him at this time. He was a tall thin man, but he tried to keep fit as much as possible, and his body was lean and muscular.

But he wanted to be king himself, and as the cat became lazier and fat, he would soon have his chance. He looked over at the other spiked haired man he was thin and was only a kid. He was day dreaming of becoming king when the horde of zombies came round the tent at them.

The thin kid screamed as a zombie bit into his cheek and he ran, but ran straight into another zombie which grabbed hold of him, and pulled him down. The tall spiky haired man was in shock, and watched as his mate was eaten by the zombies, they began to pull out his intestines as he screamed!

Two zombies grabbed the tall man, and he too cried out as one bit into his arm he dropped his gun.

He hit one zombie in the mouth, and looked in horror as he pulled his hand away and saw teeth embedded in it, blood pooling round the teeth.

"Fuck," he cursed and went down under an army of the living dead.

==

The crazy old woman was stirring the stew pots when the zombies attacked. She was in her eighties, and was regarded as the mother to most of the tribe. She was as crazy as a loon and she thought of herself as a witch, and had made various potions, but no one would ever take them. But she was always friendly to folk, and that was why they liked her so much plus she could cook. She was looking forwards to being nanny for the two new kids the little girl was so cute.

She saw the dead surrounding her as she stirred.

"You will not have my stew damn you," she cursed at them. She hit one with the large ladle and a split went up the side of its head, but it kept coming. She screamed as she was pulled to the ground the things ripping at her flesh, the stew ignored.

==

The king stood behind his men as they battled with the zombies, but they were fighting a losing battle. The zombies would soon be through his line of men, and at him the king could not have that. There was a car close by it was a white mini.

"Get that car over here now solider."

One of his men nodded, and raced over to the car and jumped in before the zombies noticed him. He started the car and drove it through a gap in the fighting men and zombies. One painted man had his throat ripped out, and blood splattered the window screen as the mini passed. The king had to get out of here, and fuck his army he would go and build another camp somewhere safer, and gather a new army.

"Here king jump in."

"No, you get out I will drive."

The man got out and the king pushed him hard, and he fell amongst the fighting men. The king got into the car and locked the doors he was sweating badly, and shaking. His big belly pushed against the steering wheel, and he had to move the seat back. He screamed out loud as he went forwards in the car hitting some of his men as he went, he no longer cared.

"Hey you fucker," one man cursed as the king flipped a man over the roof. Another man smashed one side window with his gun, and spat at the king and said, "Traitor."

But the king didn't care he was scared and drove at the metal fence the car hit the fence, and pulled it down more zombies came into the camp. The king lost control of the car, and it flipped over onto its roof the wheels spinning the engine still running. The king had no seat belt on and he lay at an odd angle his neck hurt like hell, and blood was pouring out of a cut above his right eye. The windows were all smashed, and he screamed as the dead crawled into the car, he was helpless to fight them off.

==

Stacy holding the kid's hands entered the woods, but soon they could hear the screams from the camp as the zombies attacked 'serves them right' she thought.

They stopped for a while and then continued to walk they found a village later that day, and holed up inside an old cottage for the night. The cottage was falling apart, but the door seemed strong, and anyway it was only for one night the inside of the cottage smelt of piss. They had no food or water and Stacy prayed that they would find some tomorrow in the village.

The next day they went searching and managed to find some tinned food and bottled water, but there wasn't much. Stacy put the rucksack over her shoulder with the tinned food and water inside at least they could eat something now. As they walked past one cottage Stacy saw a man looking out at them from a window.

"Hey mister," she shouted waving at the man in the window.

"Come on kids there is a man over there."

"How can you be sure that he is alive?" Jake asked.

"I'm scared," Lucy said.

"Come on and we will find out maybe he has food."

Stacy knocked on the front door.

The front garden was well kept and the flower beds looked good.

"Go away."

"Mister please we have no food or shelter," Stacy pleaded.

"Not my problems now fuck off."

"Please help us."

"If you don't move in two minutes, I will shoot you dead all three of you."

Then a gun barrel came out of the letter box.

"But I have kids with me."

"I can see that you cunt now fuck off or I shoot."

"Fuck you," Stacy cursed and held onto the kid's hands, and walked away from the cottage.

Chapter twenty

Hadley

"Bloody bastards," the old man cursed as he watched the woman and two kids walk back down his garden path. Hadley was a mean old bastard, and had been his whole life he was mean to his wife until she died of a heart attack two years ago. He had treated her like a slave, and he had never cooked a meal in his life until she passed away. How she had stayed with him was a mystery, and her family told him at the funeral that she deserved a medal for all the shit he had given her. But he had just smiled at them, and walked away fuck them all.

He was a tall skinny man with grey hair, and cheeks that went inwards. He had hard black eyes and a flat nose a fight in his youth over a girl, and he had come second best. People used to think he was a boxer, but he had never stepped into the ring. He held the rifle in his hands, and watched until it was clear, he would have shot them all as well. He had been lucky so far in the fact that the zombies seemed to leave him alone he made as little noise as possible.

But now these people had drawn the zombies to his house he could see them walking down the street to see what the talking had been. He had even managed to sneak out some days, and keep his garden in good order. He was running low on food, and didn't know what he would do when it ran out.

He was used to being alone even when he was married, he would spend most of his time out or in his study. He hated the fact that people, just because the world had gone to shit wanted to join up. He hated people before the outbreak, and he hated them even more now all they were was zombie fodder. He looked over his front garden at the lovely well kept flower beds, and sobbed the zombies would come in and trample them.

==

It didn't take long as he stood and watched at the window the zombies came into his garden. There were about five of them and they trampled over his flower beds, and started to bang on the front door. Damn that woman and them bloody kids he thought. One zombie came up close to the living room window, and he saw the deep wound in its cheek, and the rotting flesh which was starting to peel off. It opened its mouth, and moaned showing its blackened teeth. Another zombie trod on his flowers it only had one arm and a massive hole in its throat dried blood covered its shirt.

A woman zombie wearing a night gown her hair all fizzy, and her jaw missing, and three fingers on her out stretched hand.

"Fuck you do you know how long it took me to keep that garden good."

He shouted the words the zombies were here so what the hell, "You are all ugly bastards."

As he watched more zombies came down the road and headed for the cottage.

"Come on why don't you all join the fucking party."

==

Hadley took the last bottle of whisky out of his drink cabinet he had always kept it well stocked, but now he was down to the last bottle. He poured himself a large one and drank it neat. He raised his glass in the air and said, "Fuck it."

He sat down in his favourite chair, and looked at the blank television screen.

He missed his television he was a fan of game shows and he loved to watch *tipping point* and *pointless*.

"To game shows," and he took another long sip. The truth be known he missed his late wife a little bit. She had been a damned good cook, and he missed that, and she had kept the house clean and tidy he missed that too. He had lived on take aways and micro wave foods until the outbreak of course, and then he had lived on tinned food.

"Too my late wife damn she was a good cook."

He took a gulp of the whisky and heard the zombies pounding on the front door he was talking loudly he didn't care anymore. He remembered his wife begging to go away on holiday with or without him, but he would never allow that and holidays were just a waste of money. She had asked him to get a car he could drive, but again a waste of money insurance was so expensive. She had to do with the bus and taxis, and unlike him who enjoyed public transport she hated it.

"Too my wife I wish she was here to keep this place tidy."

He poured another large shot into his empty glass he was starting to feel light headed already maybe because of lack of food.

==

He took a long swallow and looked at the front door, and then heard banging on the back door. Now the back door was not in good shape it was coming off the hinges he had been meaning to get the damned thing fixed for ages. But like most thongs now he just couldn't be bothered.

"Hey keep the fucking noise down you cunts."

The banging just got louder and he took another long swallow of his whisky. They had a dog once and they called it skip the thing was a menace to him always biting his ankles.

It had been a Yorkshire terrier a little black and ginger thing god he had hated it. His wife had loved the little brute and called it her baby, they had never had children thank God to that as well he hated kids.

"Fuck kids and fuck dogs."

One day while she had been at work, he had taken the thing to the park, and kicked it into the river. He saw the thing swimming and quickly made his way home, but of course the thing was waiting for him at the front door dripping wet. His wife had asked him why the dog was so dirty, and he said it fell into the river, but she didn't believe him. Anyway a few weeks later he had enough the thing never left him alone biting his ankles growling at him all the time.

So, one day he put the thing in a large plastic bag and sealed it. He threw the bag into the large waste bin in the village square, and that was that he told his wife the thing had run away.

"Fuck you skip you cunt."

Then when they retired, he had lived in the garden, and down the local pub anything to get away from her. He was almost eighty now and looked like a walking road map with his wrinkled face. The back door began to crack he heard it Cleary and drank more whisky.

"Fuck you zombies come and get me."

==

Hadley took another long swallow of whisky now he was feeling drunk as a skunk. The back door gave way and he heard the moaning get louder as the zombies headed for the living room. He was just going to sit down, and let them take him, but now he got to his feet, and picked up his rifle.

"Bastards," he spat as the first zombie came into the living room.

The thing had a scar across its nose like someone had head butted it, and its eyes were black holes. Hadley shot it in the head and it went back wards onto the carpeted floor another zombie tripped over its body, and its head crashed onto the wall. It was dazed, but was still trying to get back to its feet the other zombies started to step over the body, and come into the living room.

Hadley took aim at a woman zombie she wore a business suit that was dirty and blood stained. She had short dark hair and her nose was missing, and one of her ears had been ripped off. He shot her in the neck and then aimed higher and shot her in the forehead just like the television reporter had said to do. Hadley needed to reload he only had three bullets in the chamber. He had no time plus he was drunk, and he sat back down in his chair as the zombies piled into the room.

He screamed as they started to rip off his flesh in chunks and stuff it into their mouths. He cried out as zombie's bit into his face and arms he moaned as his life blood ran out of his old thin body.

Chapter twenty-one

Crazy rubbish tip man

The two men wearing army outfits moved down the street of the small village. Parker was twenty-nine, and had never been in the army they had found the gear in the back of a jeep along with two rifles and ammo. He was of medium height with short brown hair, and a thin bony face. Douglas was the same height, but a bigger man with a belly that stuck out. He too was twenty-nine, and he and Parker were like brothers before the outbreak, and after always looking out for each other. Finding the army gear had been a god send and unlike Parker Douglas had been in the army before. Be it only briefly he had hated the army life, and in the end bought himself out.

The two men saw the cottage and moved in closer they saw a couple of zombies banging on the front door, but these soon followed the rest round the back. Parker went into the front garden followed by Douglas, and they looked into the living room window.

"Holy shit," Parker said and looked away.

Douglas looked and said, "Damn that is so gross."

The old man was just a skeleton with bits of flesh hanging off the bone, the zombies had really gone to town on his corpse.

"Come on let's get out of here," Parker said moving off.

"I'm with you brother."

==

The rubbish tip man smiled as a zombie came into the rubbish tip the sound of the birds probably brought it in. There were always birds hunting through the piles of waste. The rubbish dump was surrounded by a brick wall, but it was broken in some places, and the wall was old and crumbled. The dump had been used regularly before the outbreak, and so it was full of rubbish and waste food.

The smell was bad, but rubbish tip man liked his home and was used to the smell. He didn't eat the waste no he used it as camouflage he often went hunting in the town for tinned food. The zombies if they came into the dump never bothered him, he was covered in the smell of waste. They only went for the smell of warm human flesh.

Walter Hamilton had been a successful businessman in his day, and had made loads of money only to lose it all on booze and drugs. Then he had been free and easy sleeping with hundreds of women. But the good times had come to an end, and he had been a down and out when the outbreak happened. He was now forty-five and had no hair, and a face that had not seen soap in months.

But he liked the rubbish dump and had decided to live there when the zombies appeared. He heard rumours that you had to shoot them in the head, and never be caught in the cities the dead owned the cities. But here things were fine, and the zombies left him well alone. The two army men came into the rubbish dump, and the rubbish tip man was out in the open.

His home was underground he had dug a hole and put a roof over, and inside were some old furniture he had found.

"Hey you what the fuck are you doing here."

The rubbish tip man sighed, and walked over to the two men.

The zombie was walking over to them as well. One of the men took out a knife and approached the zombie, and put the blade into its head.

"Who are you this is my place fuck off?" the rubbish tip man tried to sound hard, but it didn't work he had a squeaky voice.

"Fuck you old man," Parker said and pointed his rifle at the dirty man.

"Hey no need for guns," the rubbish tip man held up his hands.

The other man came back and looked at the dirty man.

"What the fuck is this," he laughed.

"You might laugh young man, but the zombies leave me well alone."

Parker grunted and replied, "Yes because you smell so bad."

==

The rubbish tip man smiled at the two army men and said, "I'm glad you are here because I know what is going to happen."

"What's going to happen old man," Parker asked him.

"Do you live here in this dump," Douglas butted in.

"Of course, I do I'm the rubbish tip man, and the zombies leave me be."

"Man, you are crazy," Douglas replied.

Parker looked at his mate and said again, "So what is going to happen old man?"

The rubbish tip man looked from one man to the other as if they were mad, "You should know being in the military."

"Just spit it out," Douglas said.

The rubbish tip man laughed and spat on the ground.

"You are going to bomb England of course, get rid of all the zombies and survivors in one hit."

"That is bullshit," Parker said as another zombie came in the dump.

"Look come and stay with me in the dump I have room for you both."

Douglas laughed, "Fuck that you crazy old bastard."

Parker aimed and shot the zombie in the head.

"Oh, great now we will have loads of them coming into the dump thanks a bunch," the old man cursed. Then he added, "You know I'm right about the bombs."

"We are not military and we don't know anything," Parker said looking around the dump.

Douglas gripped his friend's arm and said, "Come on Parker let's get out of here."

"Yes, your right, bye old man," Parker said with a smile on his face. The rubbish tip man muttered under his breath as he watched the two army men walk away.

Now more zombies came into the dump looking for the source of the noise. The rubbish tip man headed for his home he would stay inside a while until the zombies moved off, best not to be caught in a group of them.

==

Parker and Douglas got back to their jeep and started up the engine they had seen many zombies going into the dump.

"Hope the old man will be okay," Parker said looking out the window screen.

"Fuck him he was crazy," Douglas laughed.

"Yes, but I kind of felt sorry for him you know."

"Yes, well I'm sure he will be fine he smells like a god damned zombie anyway."

"Yes, your right Douglas."

With that the two men drove out of the small town, and headed into the countryside keeping away from the cities.

==

That evening the rubbish tip man was sitting outside his home looking up into the sky he was sure the army would bomb the country. The zombies had moved off after a while there was nothing very exciting for them inside the rubbish dump. A few of the zombies had come up to his home, but they had just shambled away after a while. There was no fresh smell of humans here.

"I know they will drop the bombs."

He looked round the deserted rubbish dump, and again into the night sky.

"I just know they will."

Then as he watched the night sky lit up, and the bright light shot through the night sky.

"Man, I told you," he said pointing up into the sky.

He stood up and walked back into his underground home, and waited for his impending death.

"This is it then," he said as he sat on his old bed.

But the bright light was just meteor rite falling to the earth.

The end

C Robert Paul Bennett 2015